NOODLEHEADS TAKE IT EASY

by **Tedd Arnold**
Martha Hamilton
and **Mitch Weiss**

illustrated by **Tedd Arnold**

HOLIDAY HOUSE • NEW YORK

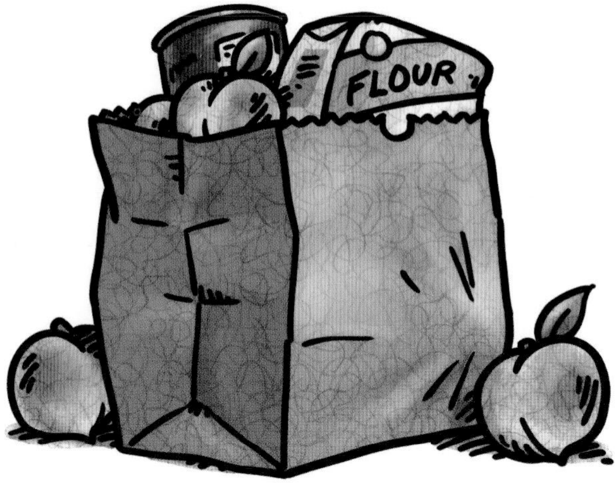
FLOUR

Specially for Layla
—T.A.

For Theo and Charlie and Kate and Eric,
who are as easy as pie to love
—M.H. & M.W.

Printed and bound in May 2022 at Toppan Leefung, DongGuan, China.
The artwork was rendered digitally using Photoshop software.
www.holidayhouse.com
First Edition
1 3 5 7 9 10 8 6 4 2

Library of Congress Cataloging-in-Publication Data is available.
ISBN: 978-0-8234-4758-9

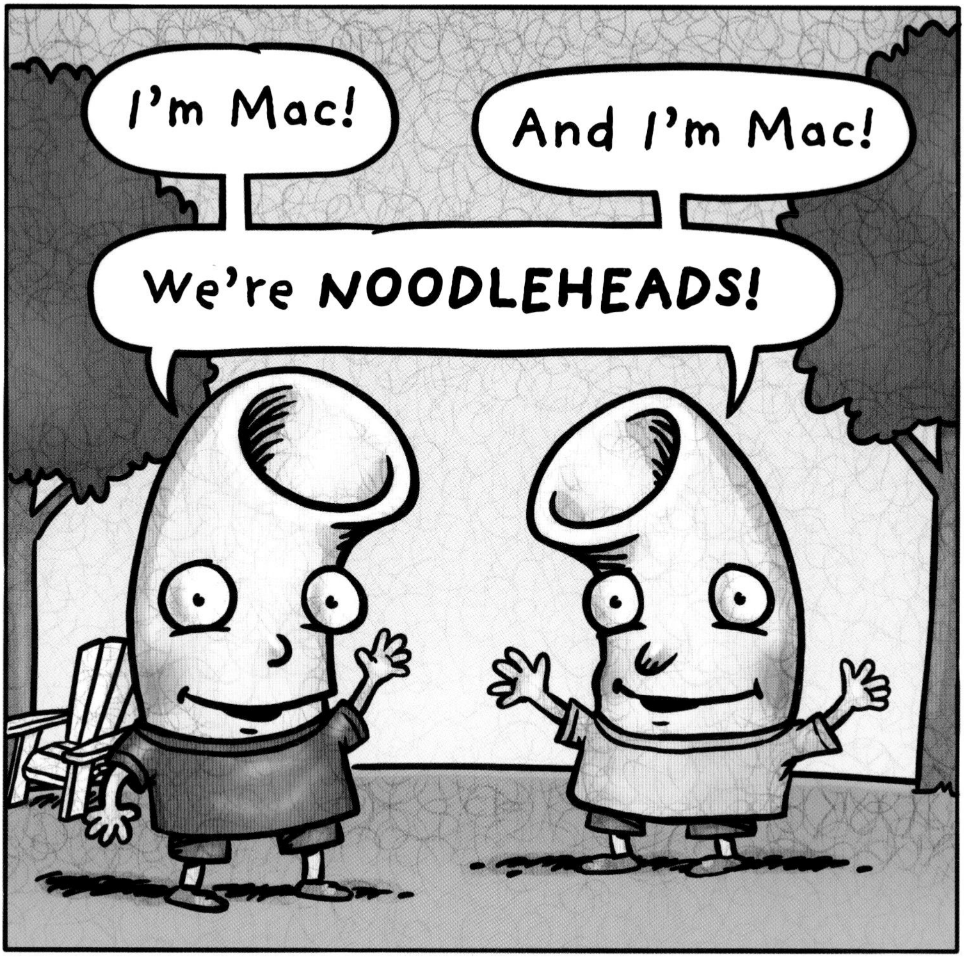
I'm Mac!
And I'm Mac!
We're NOODLEHEADS!

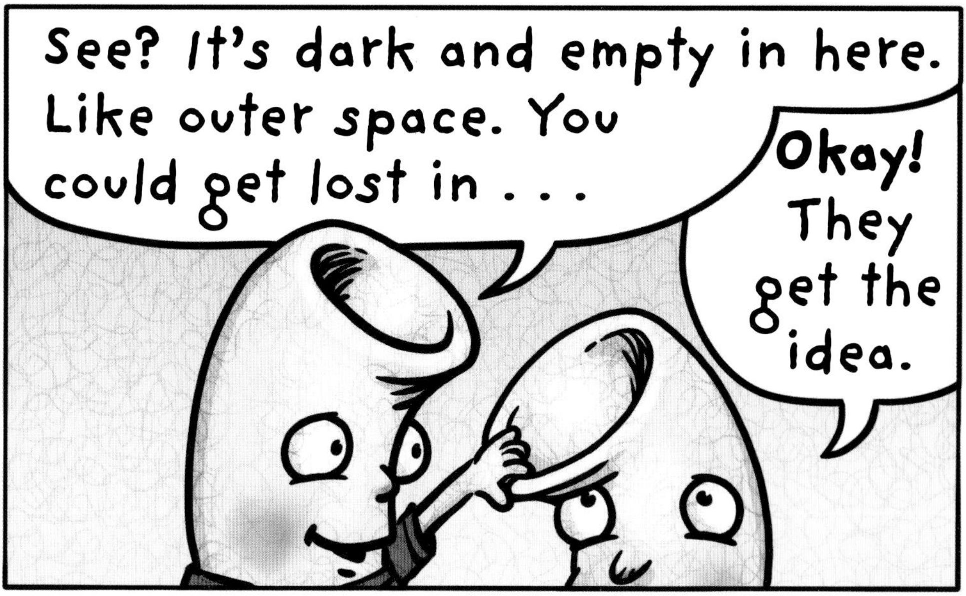
See? It's dark and empty in here. Like outer space. You could get lost in . . .
Okay! They get the idea.

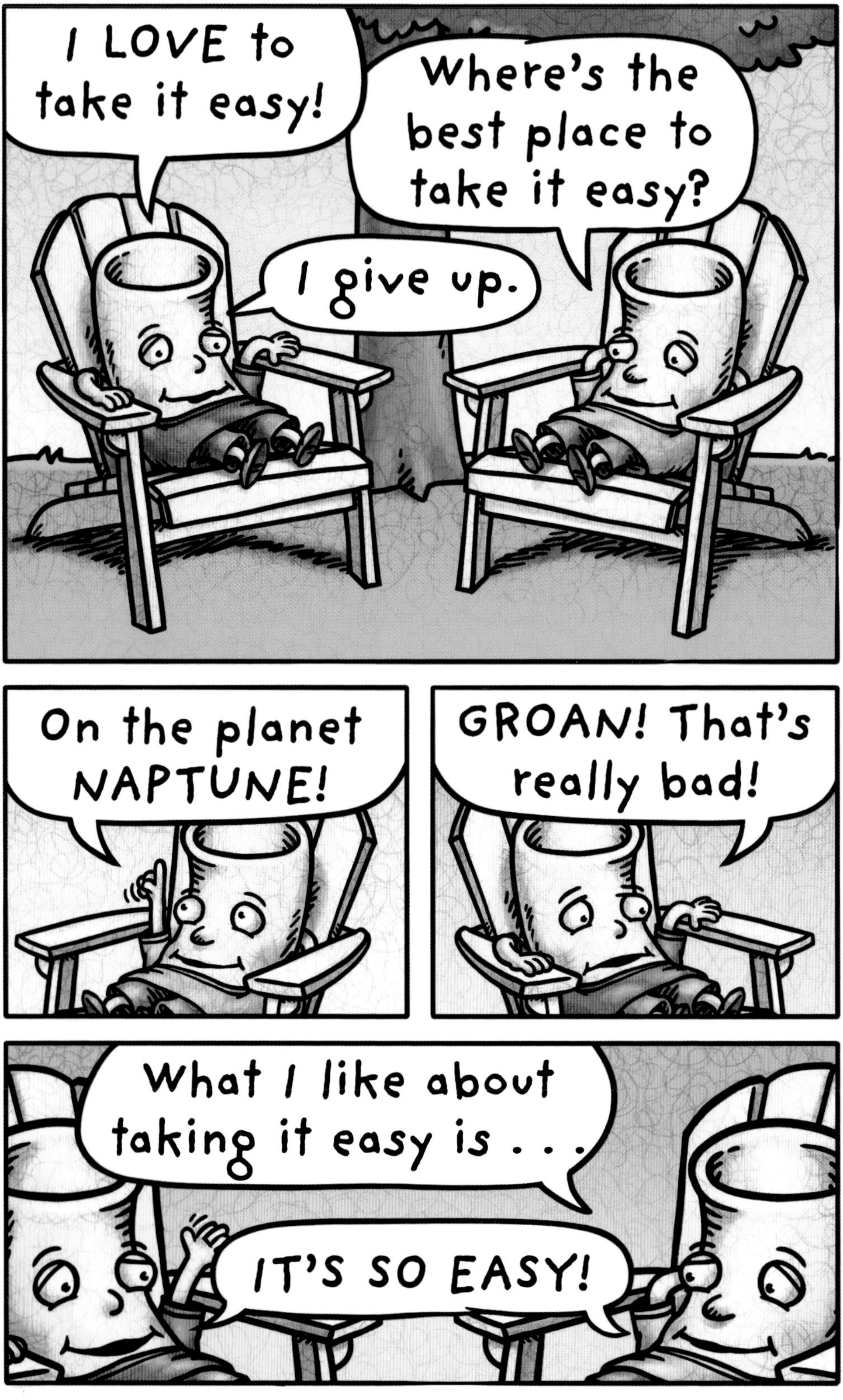
I LOVE to take it easy!
Where's the best place to take it easy?
I give up.
On the planet NAPTUNE!
GROAN! That's really bad!
What I like about taking it easy is . . .
IT'S SO EASY!

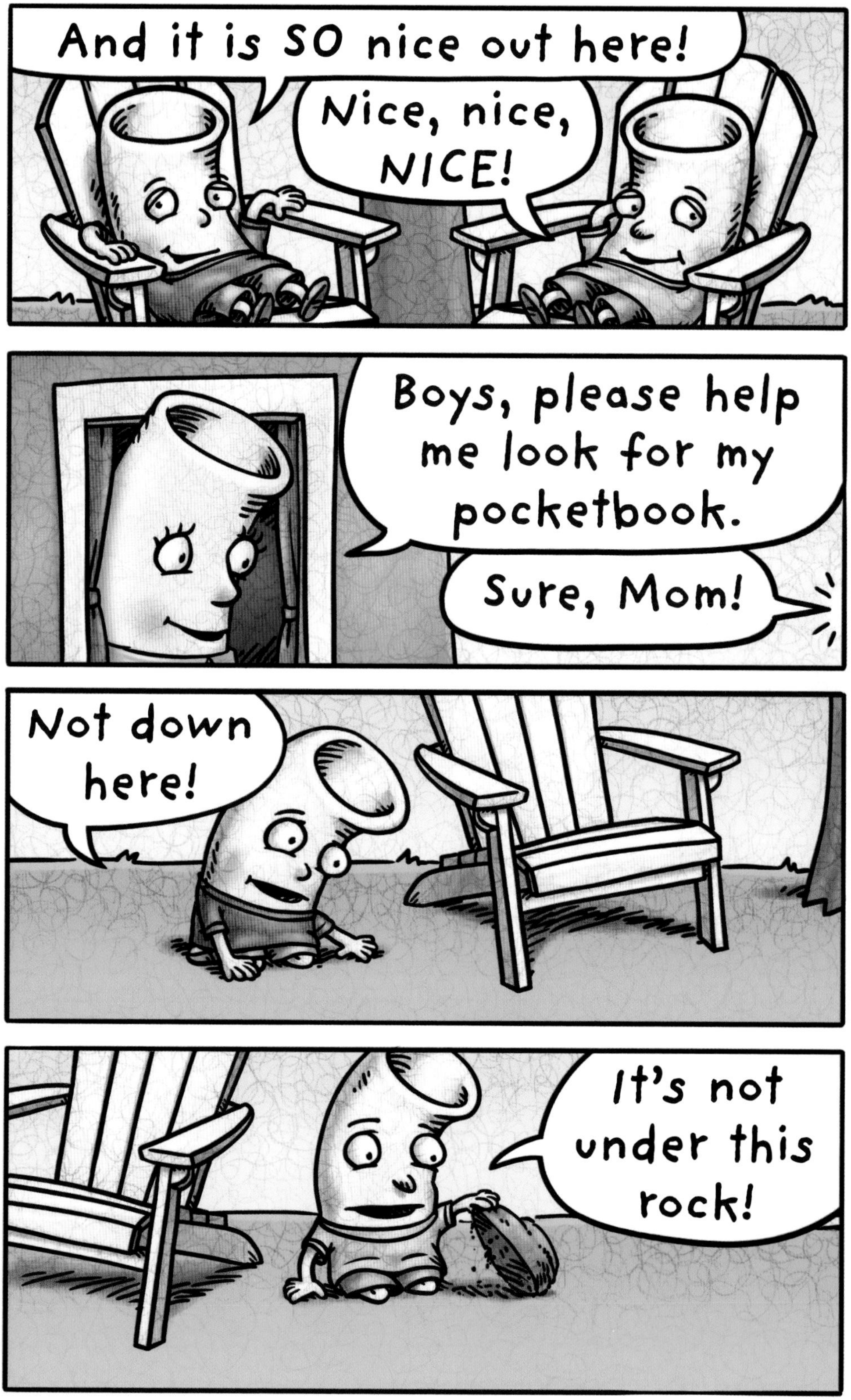
And it is SO nice out here!
Nice, nice, NICE!
Boys, please help me look for my pocketbook.
Sure, Mom!
Not down here!
It's not under this rock!

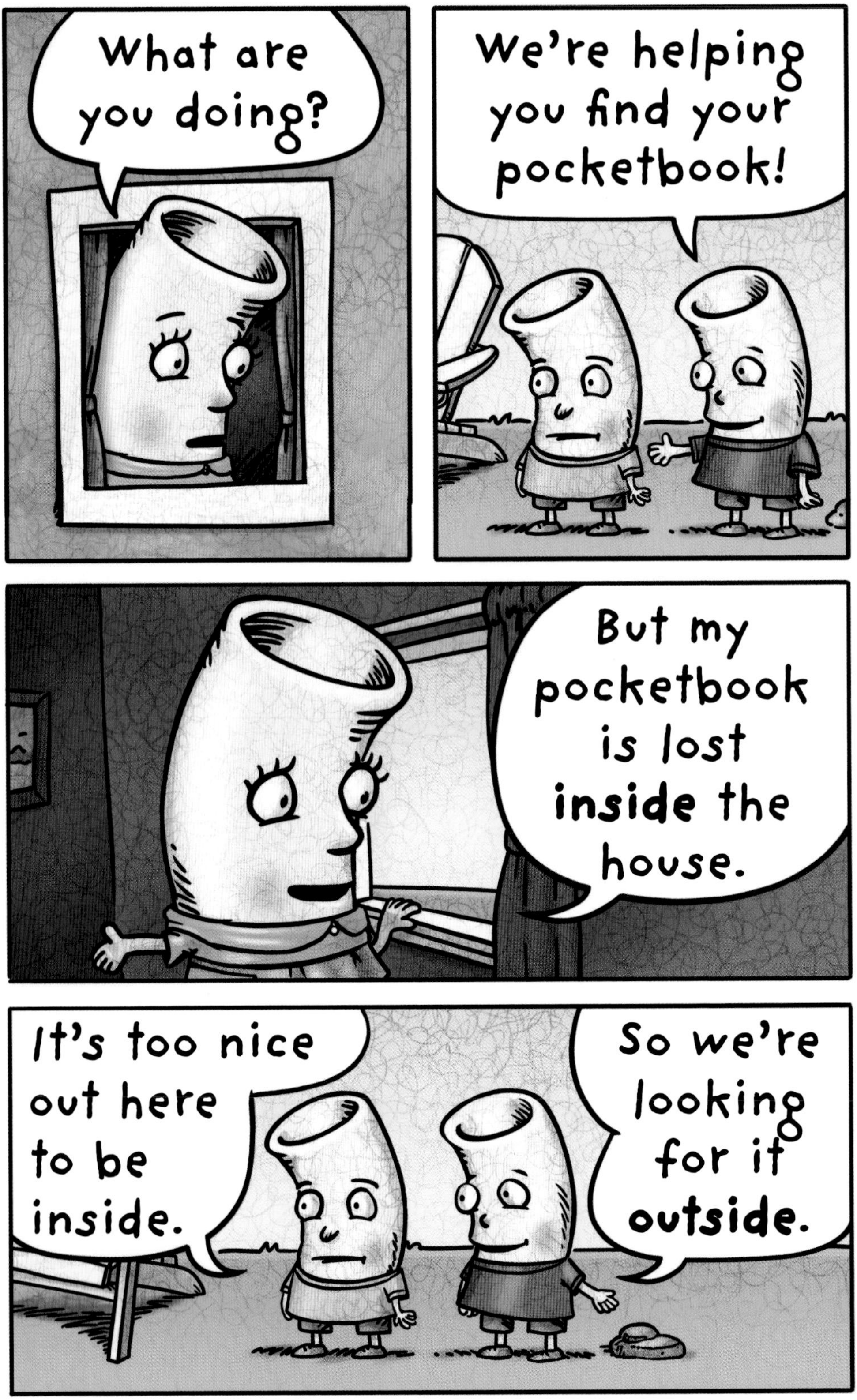
What are you doing?
We're helping you find your pocketbook!
But my pocketbook is lost **inside** the house.
It's too nice out here to be inside.
So we're looking for it **outside**.

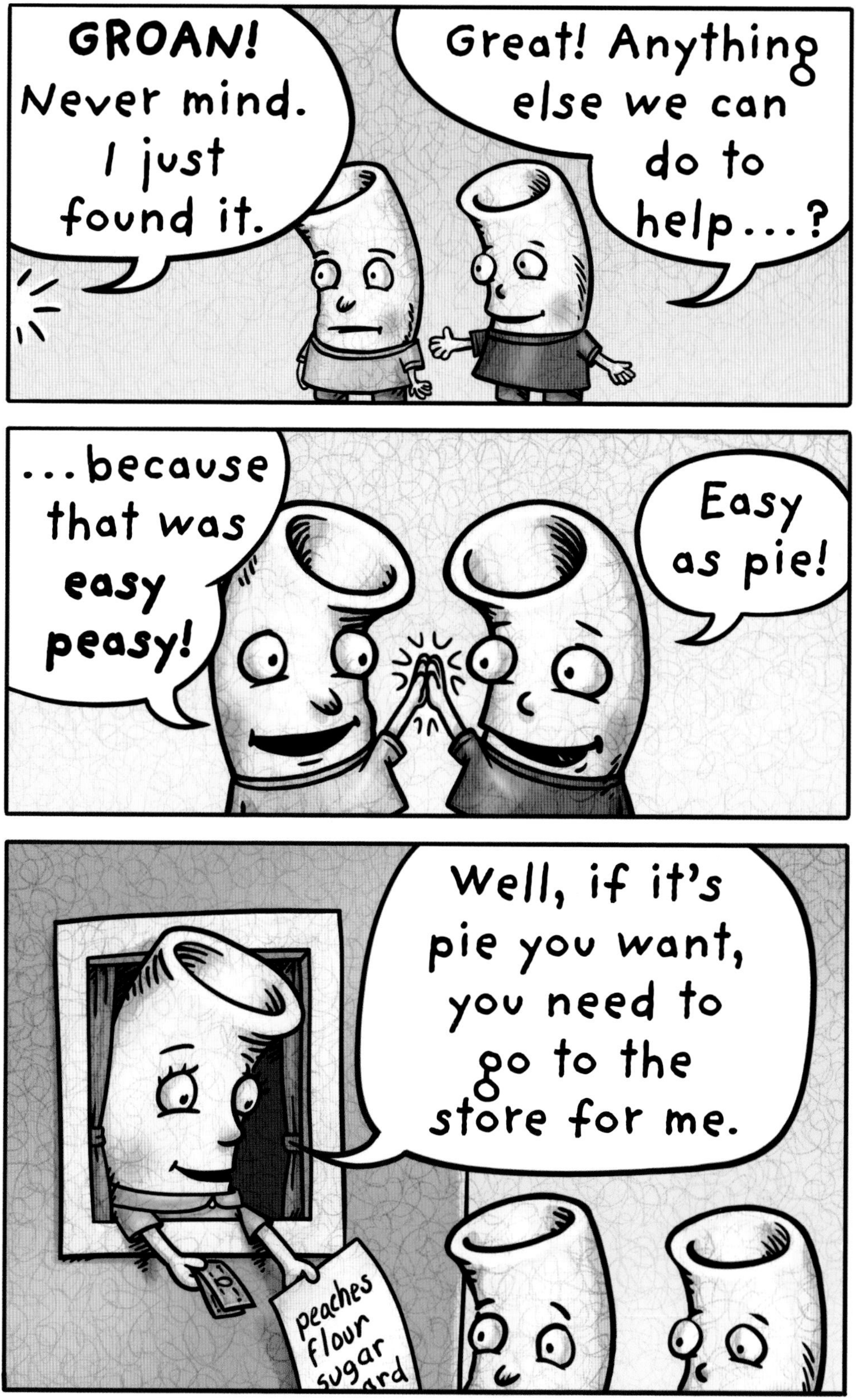
GROAN! Never mind. I just found it.
Great! Anything else we can do to help...?
...because that was easy peasy!
Easy as pie!
Well, if it's pie you want, you need to go to the store for me.
peaches
flour
sugar

NOODLEHEADS TAKE IT EASY

CHAPTER 1
EASY AS PIE???

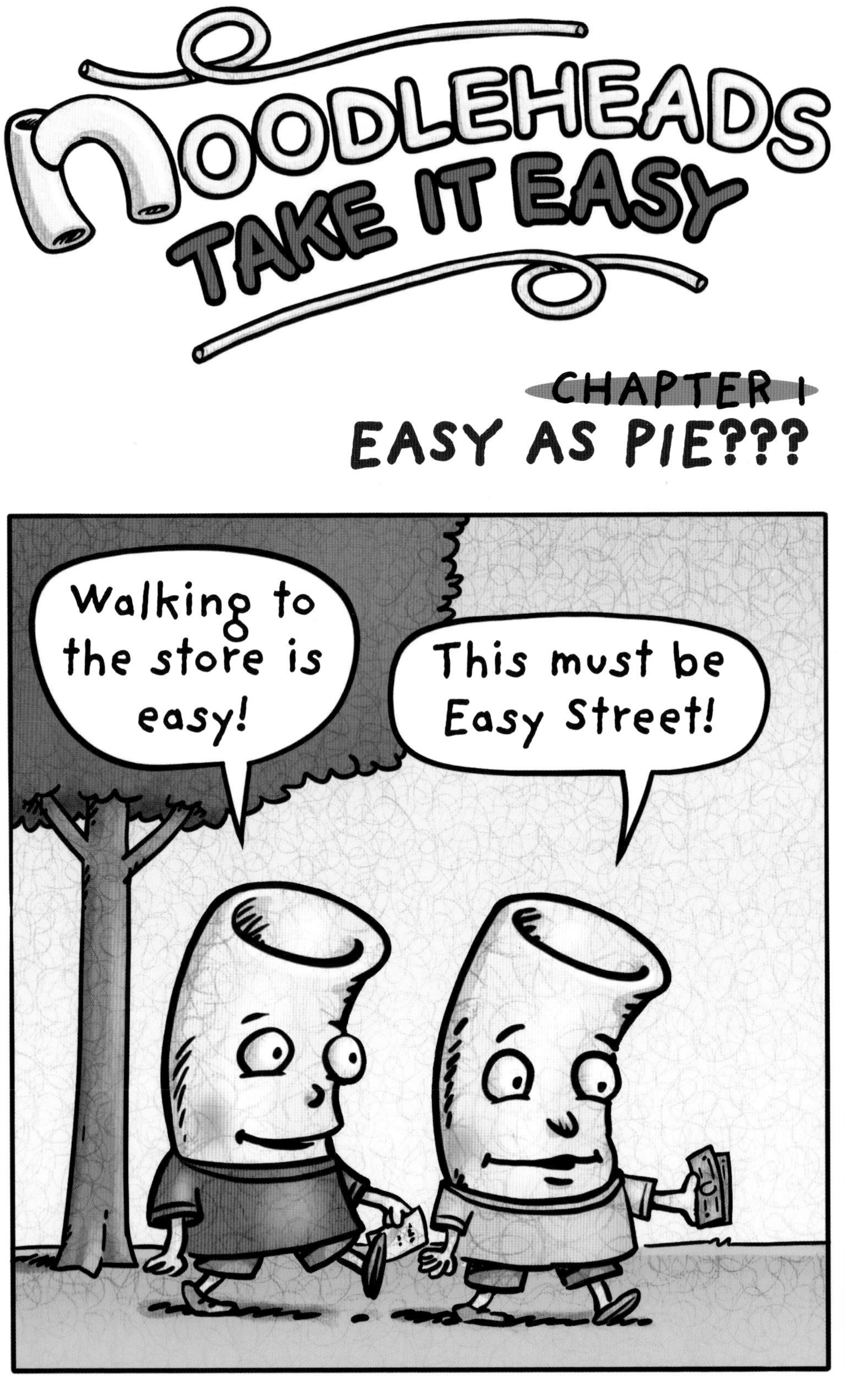

Walking to the store is easy!
This must be Easy Street!

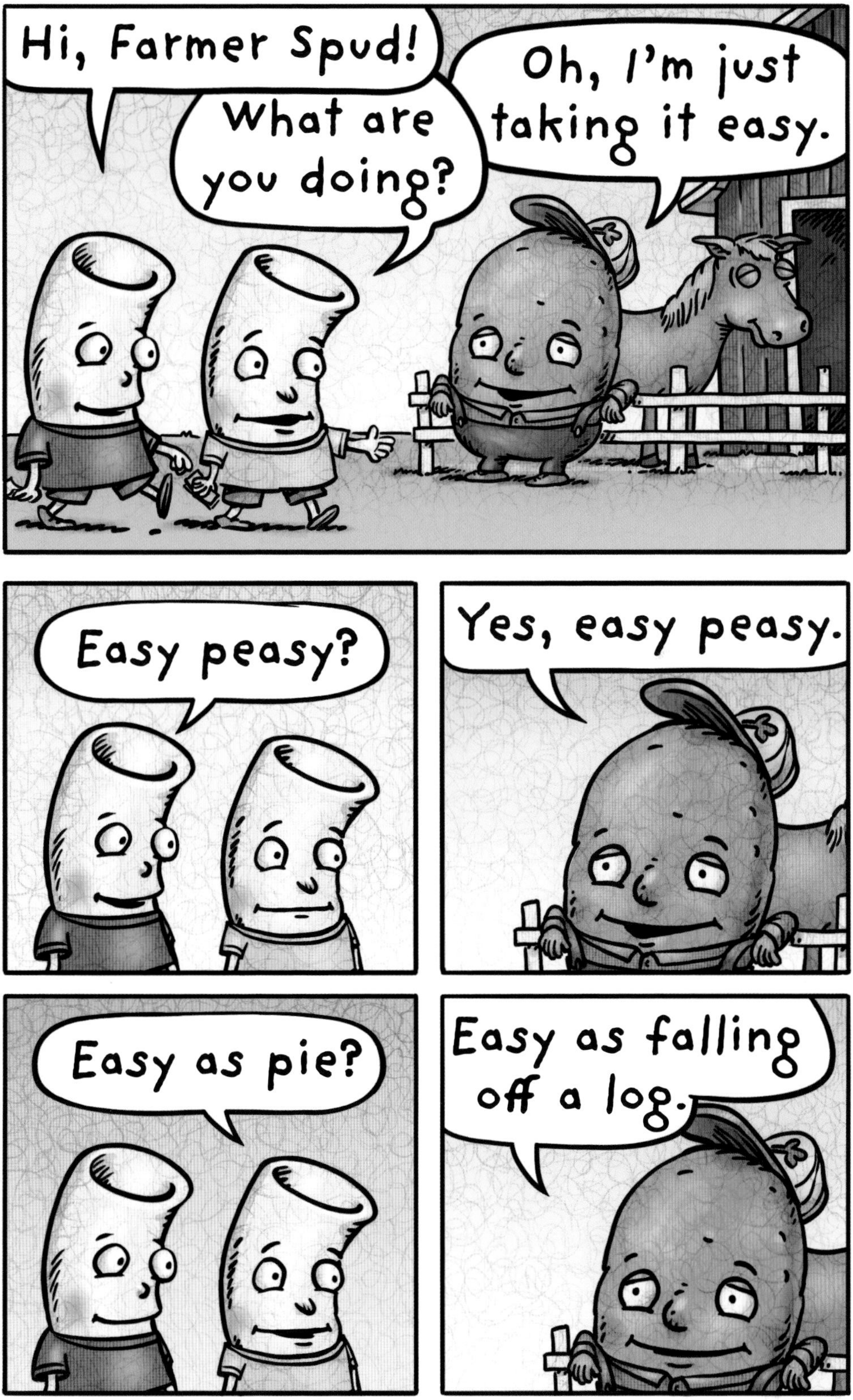
Hi, Farmer Spud!
What are you doing?
Oh, I'm just taking it easy.
Easy peasy?
Yes, easy peasy.
Easy as pie?
Easy as falling off a log.

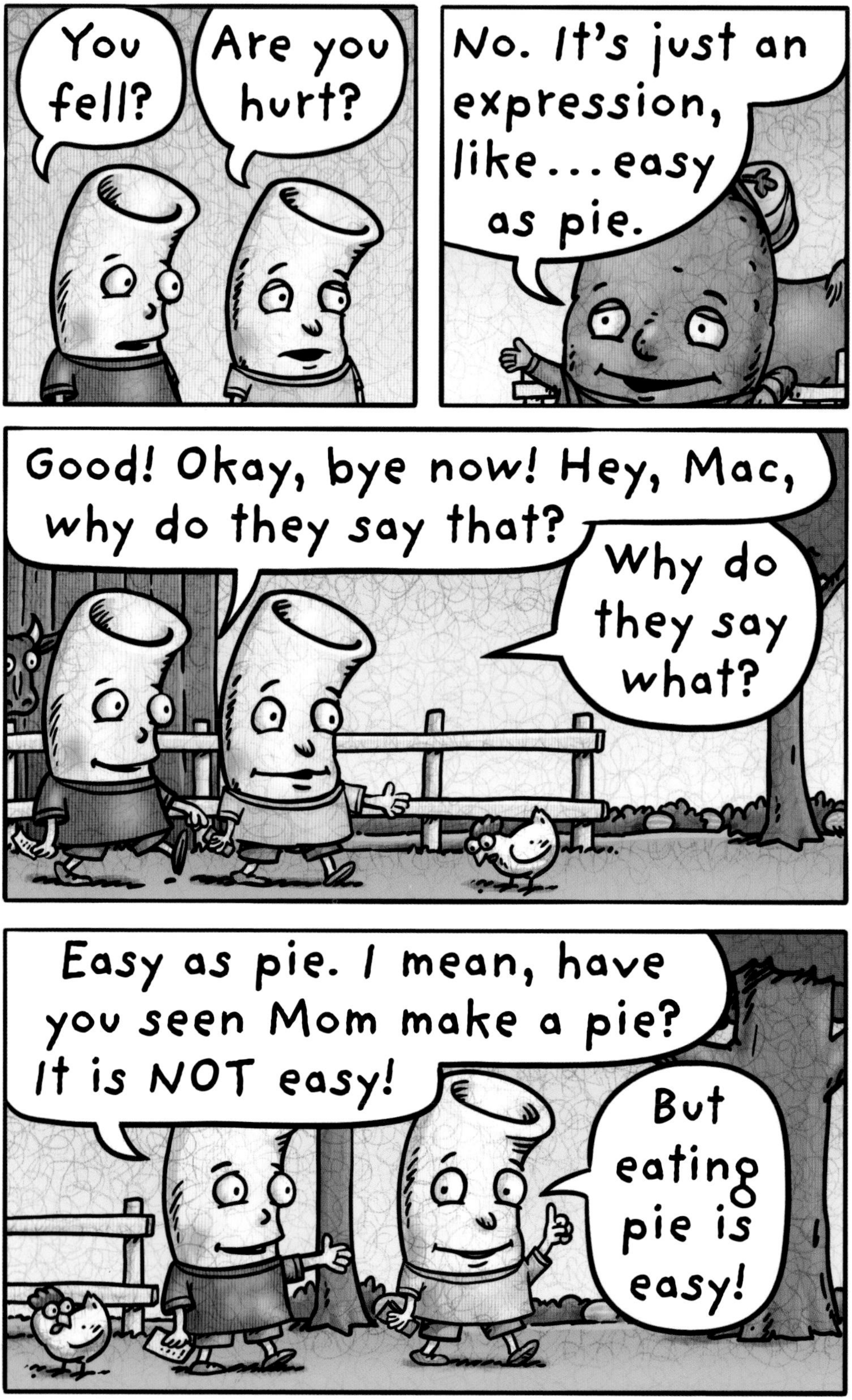
You fell?
Are you hurt?
No. It's just an expression, like... easy as pie.
Good! Okay, bye now! Hey, Mac, why do they say that?
Why do they say what?
Easy as pie. I mean, have you seen Mom make a pie? It is NOT easy!
But eating pie is easy!

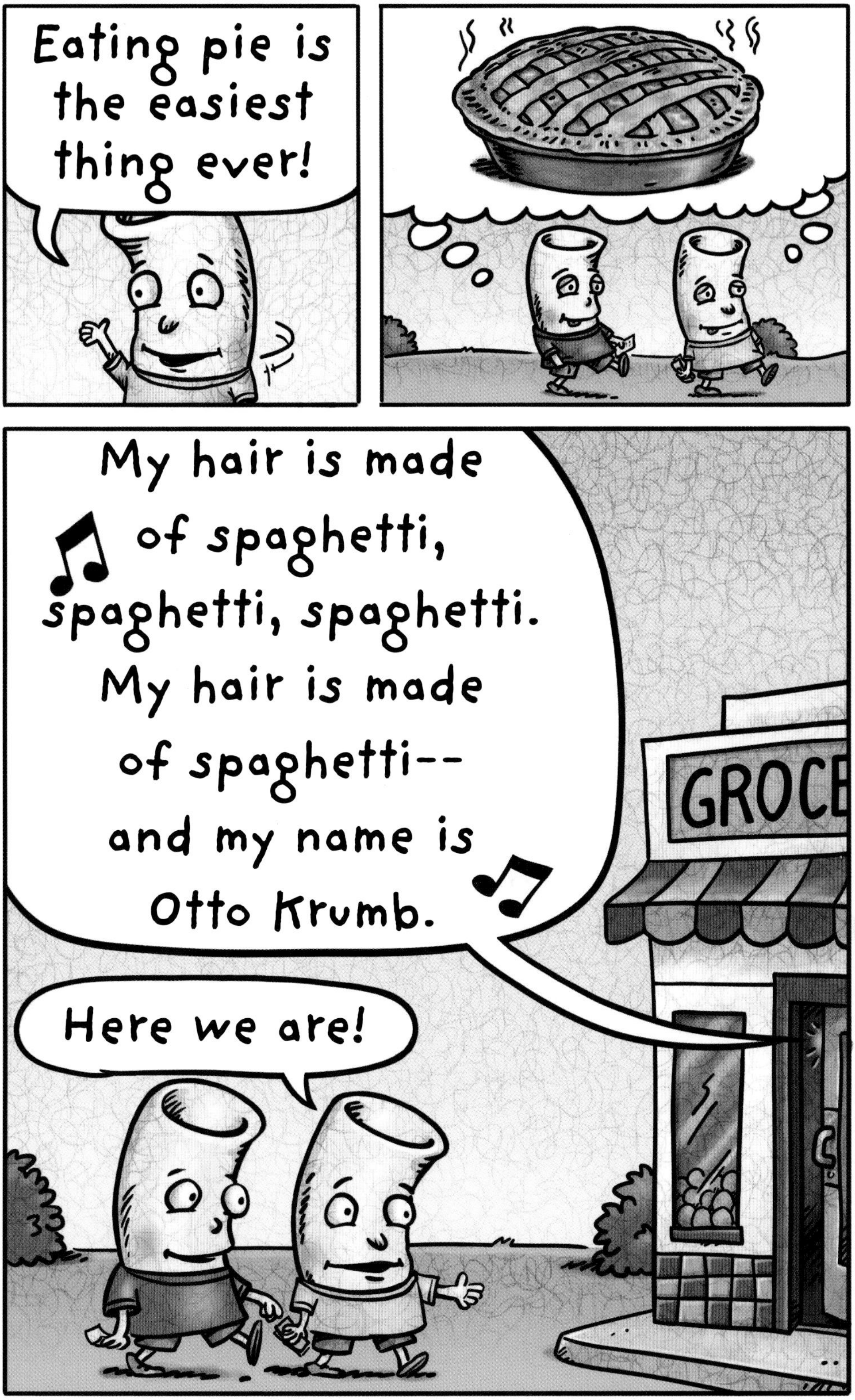
Eating pie is the easiest thing ever!
My hair is made of spaghetti, spaghetti, spaghetti. My hair is made of spaghetti-- and my name is Otto Krumb.
Here we are!

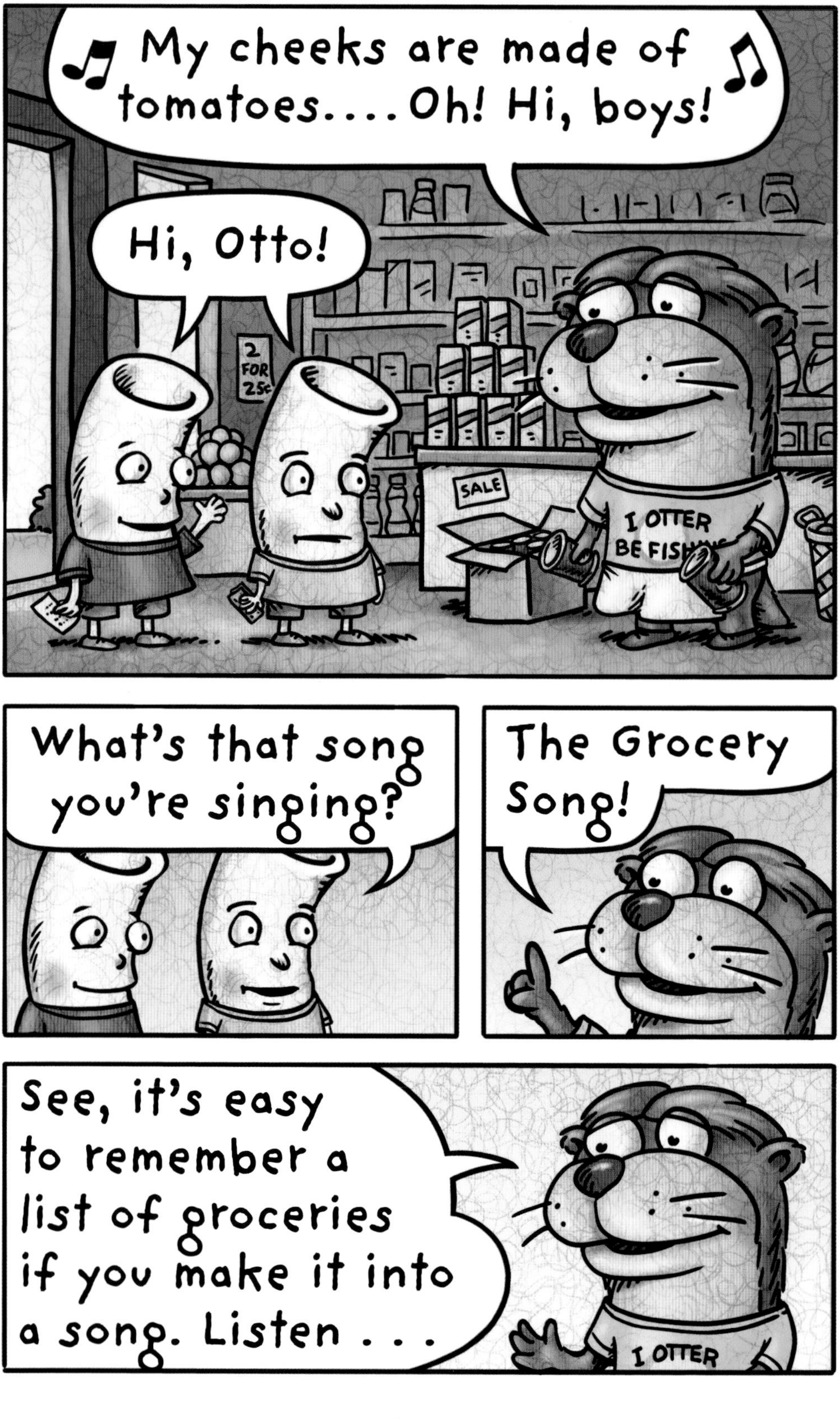
♫ My cheeks are made of tomatoes....Oh! Hi, boys! ♫
Hi, Otto!
2 FOR 25¢
SALE
I OTTER
What's that song you're singing?
The Grocery Song!
See, it's easy to remember a list of groceries if you make it into a song. Listen . . .
I OTTER

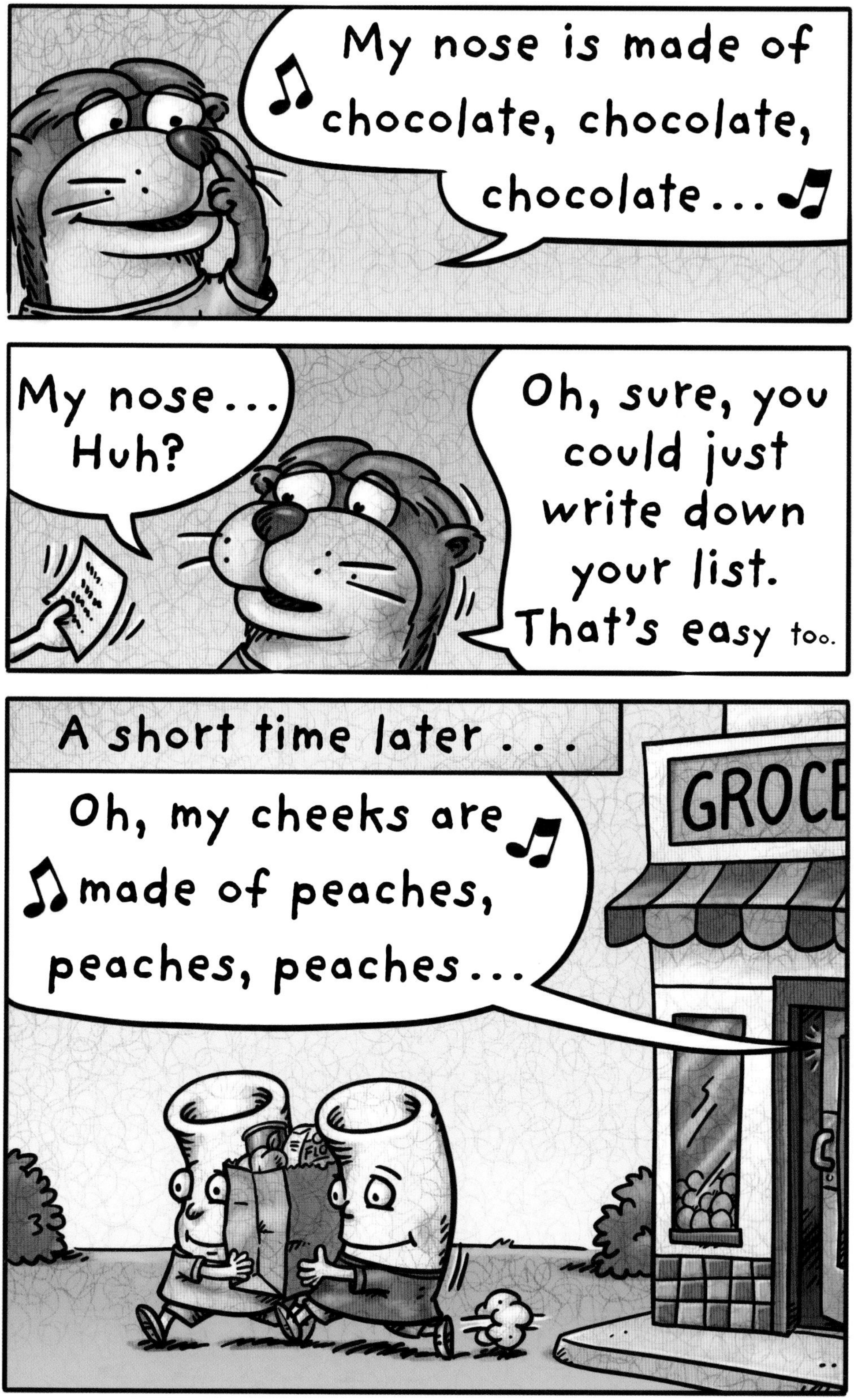
My nose is made of chocolate, chocolate, chocolate...
My nose... Huh?
Oh, sure, you could just write down your list. That's easy too.
A short time later . . .
Oh, my cheeks are made of peaches, peaches, peaches...
GROCE

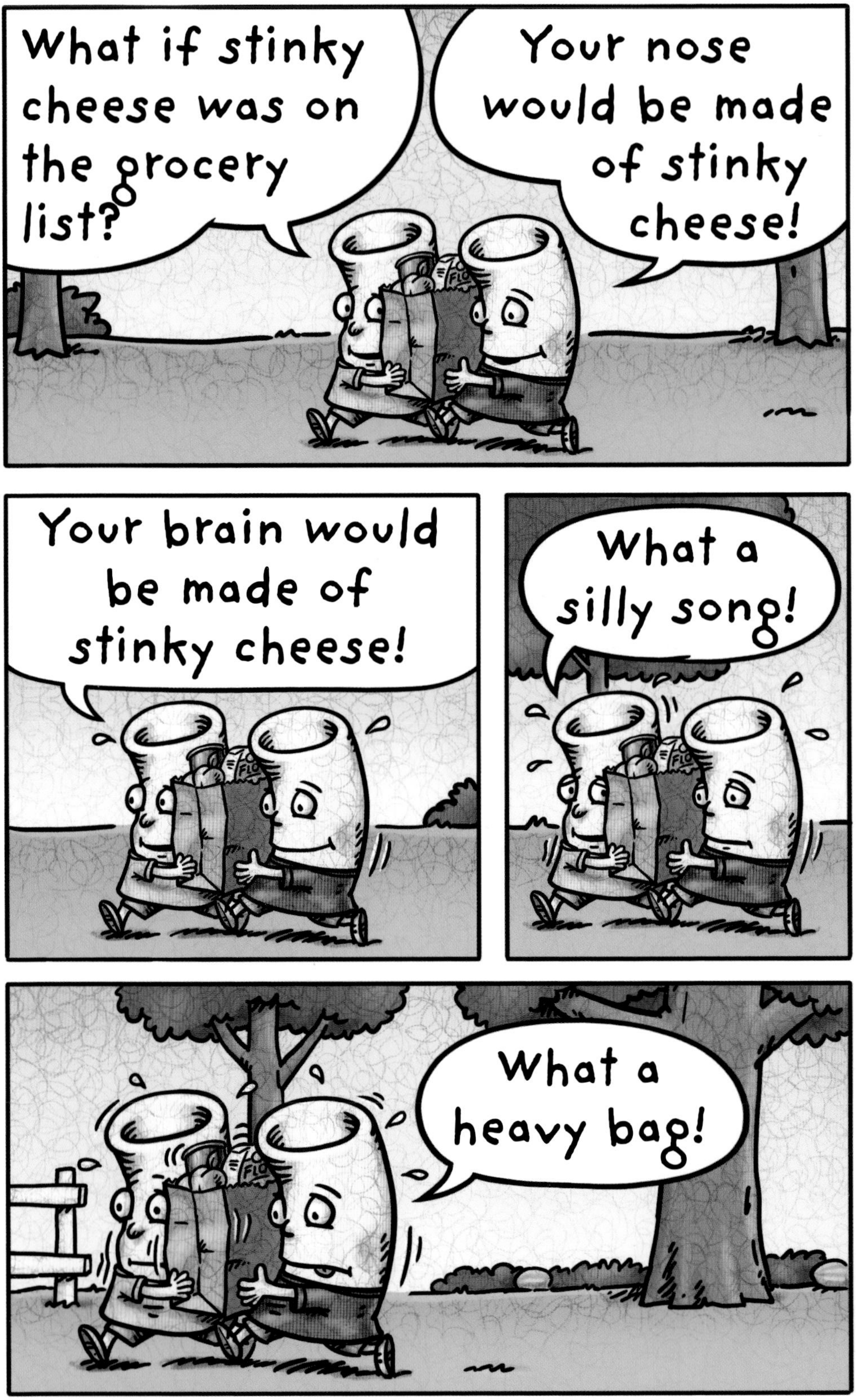
What if stinky cheese was on the grocery list?
Your nose would be made of stinky cheese!
Your brain would be made of stinky cheese!
What a silly song!
What a heavy bag!

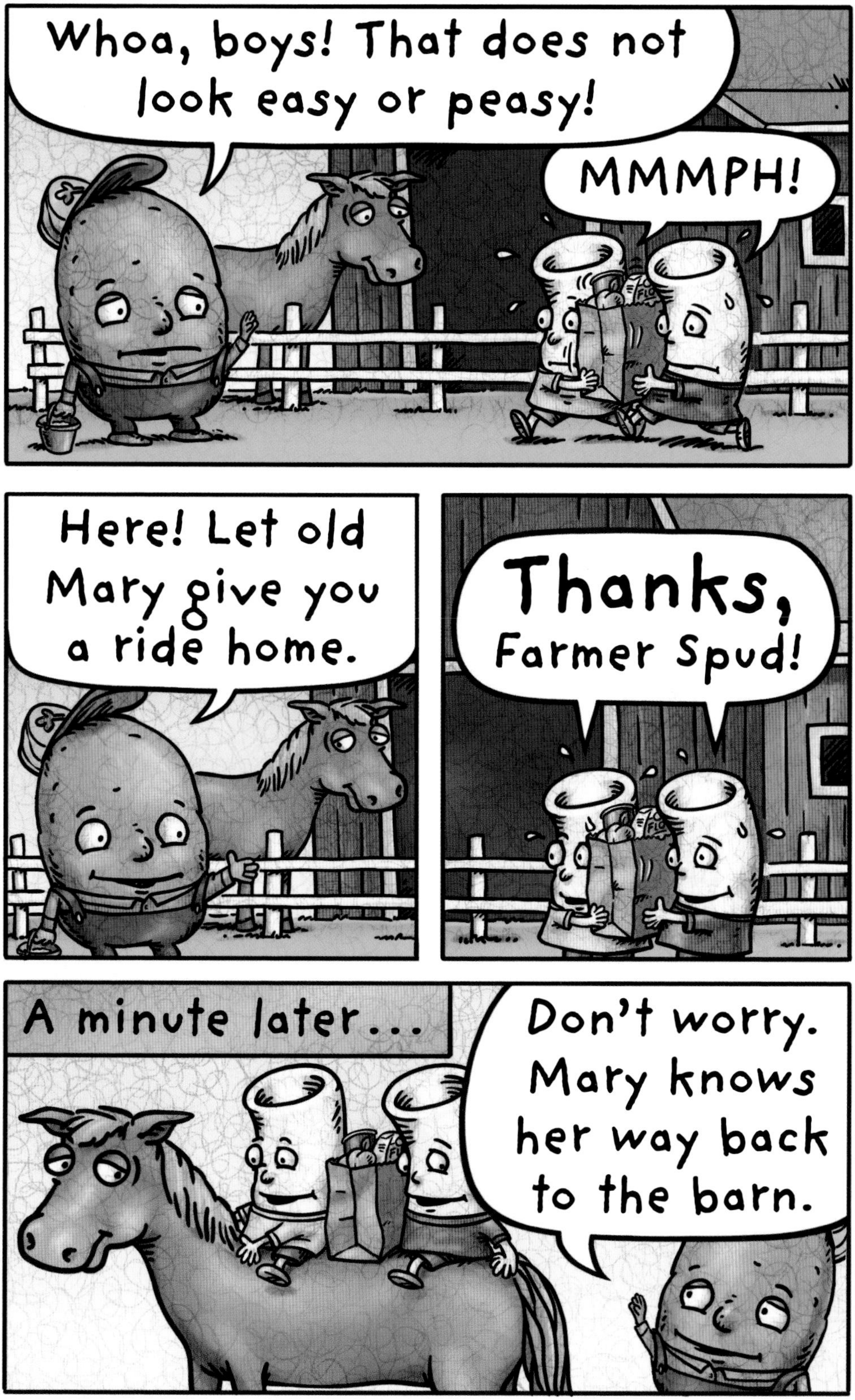
Whoa, boys! That does not look easy or peasy!
MMMPH!
Here! Let old Mary give you a ride home.
Thanks, Farmer Spud!
A minute later...
Don't worry. Mary knows her way back to the barn.

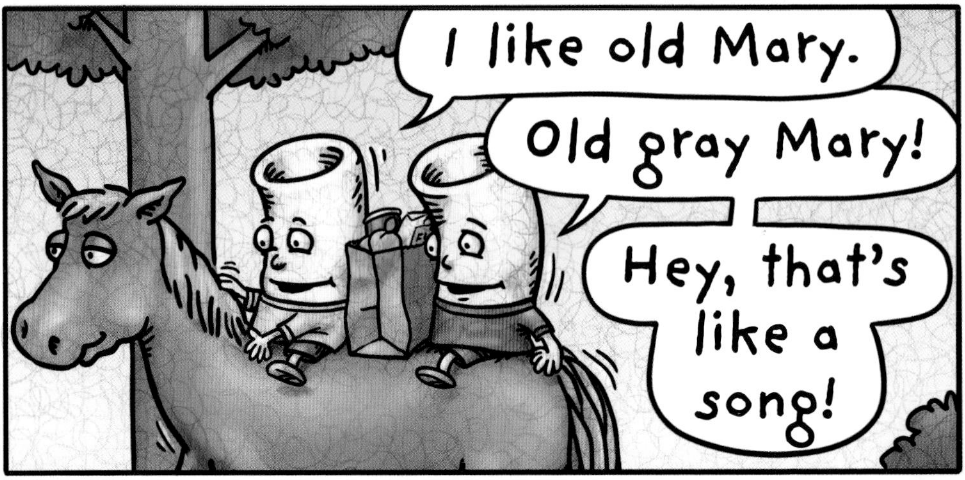
I like old Mary.
Old gray Mary!
Hey, that's like a song!

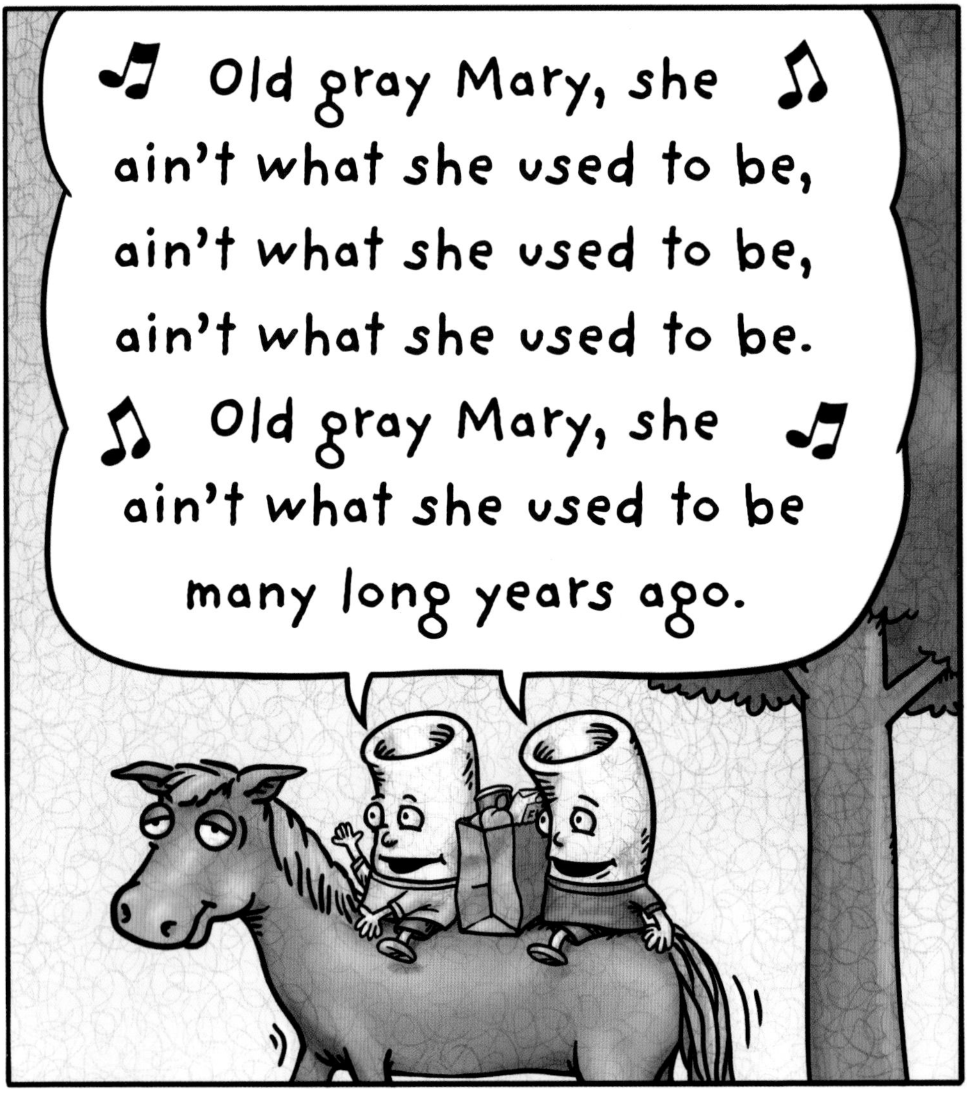
Old gray Mary, she ain't what she used to be, ain't what she used to be, ain't what she used to be. Old gray Mary, she ain't what she used to be many long years ago.

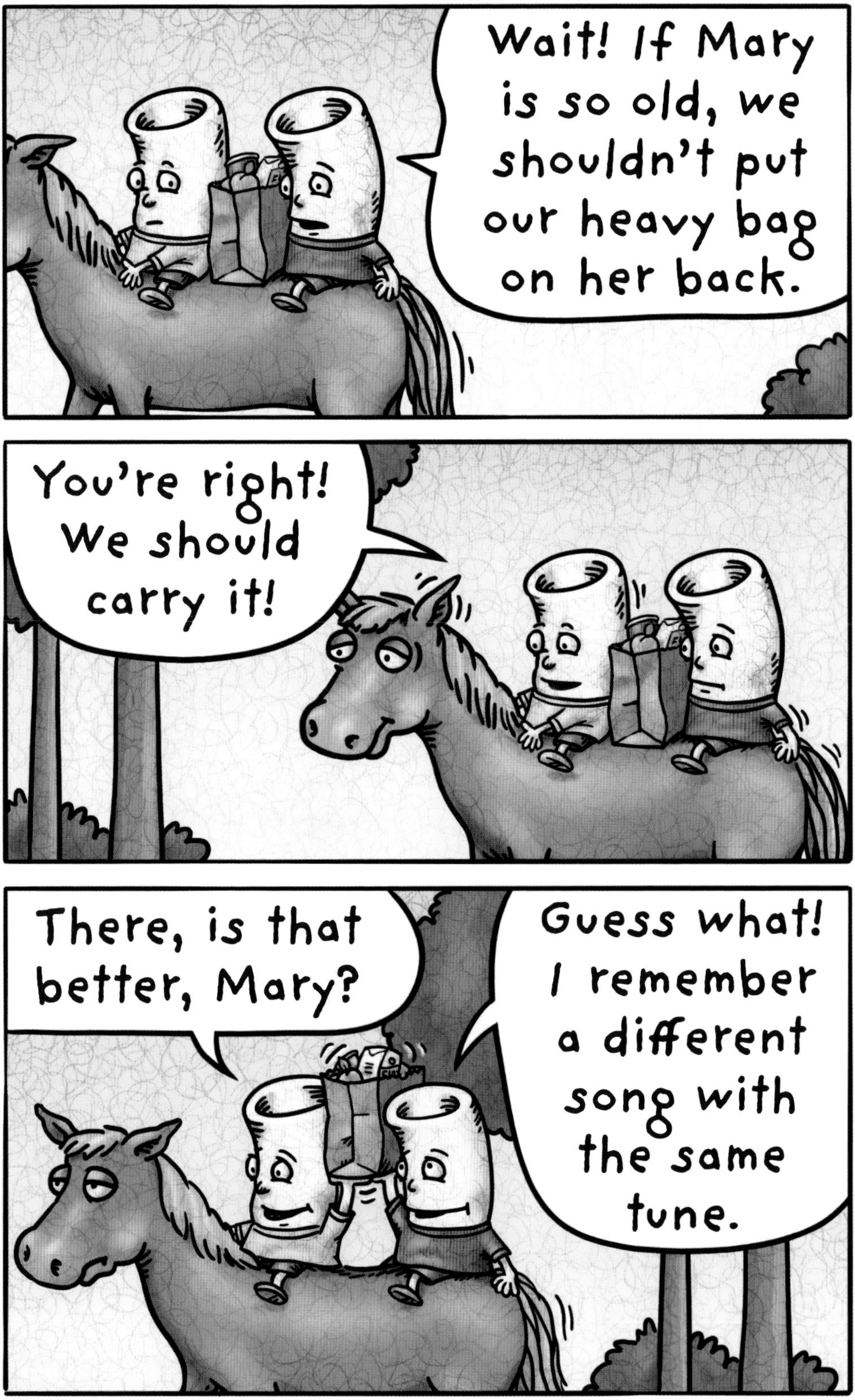
Wait! If Mary is so old, we shouldn't put our heavy bag on her back.
You're right! We should carry it!
There, is that better, Mary?
Guess what! I remember a different song with the same tune.

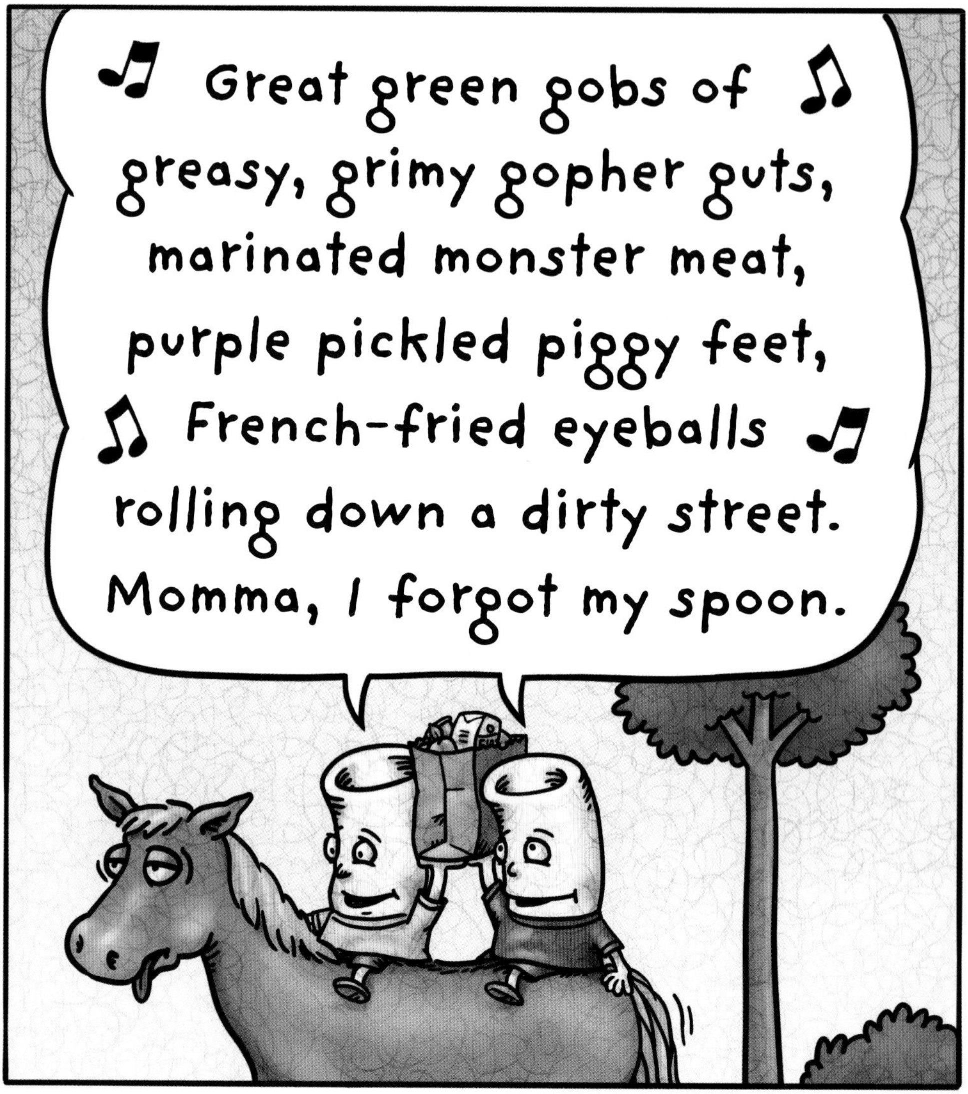
♪ Great green gobs of ♫
greasy, grimy gopher guts,
marinated monster meat,
purple pickled piggy feet,
♫ French-fried eyeballs ♪
rolling down a dirty street.
Momma, I forgot my spoon.

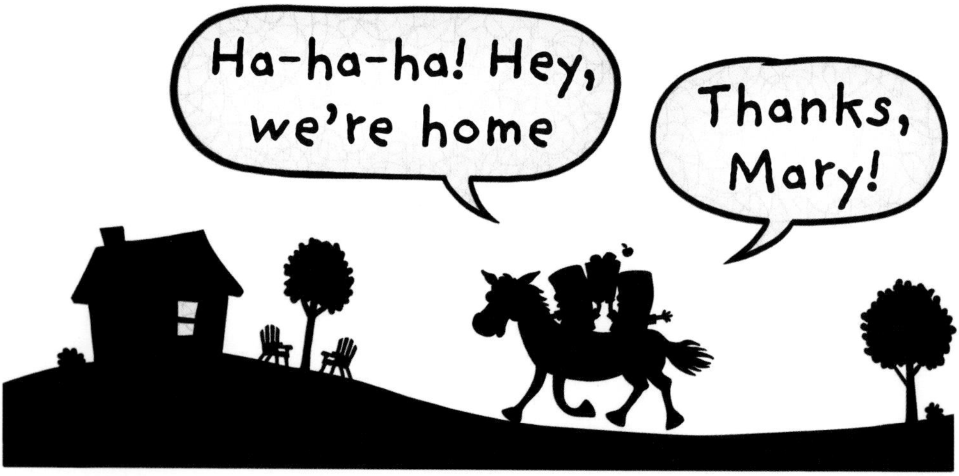
Ha-ha-ha! Hey, we're home
Thanks, Mary!

NOODLEHEADS TAKE IT EASY

CHAPTER 2
MAKING EASY HARD

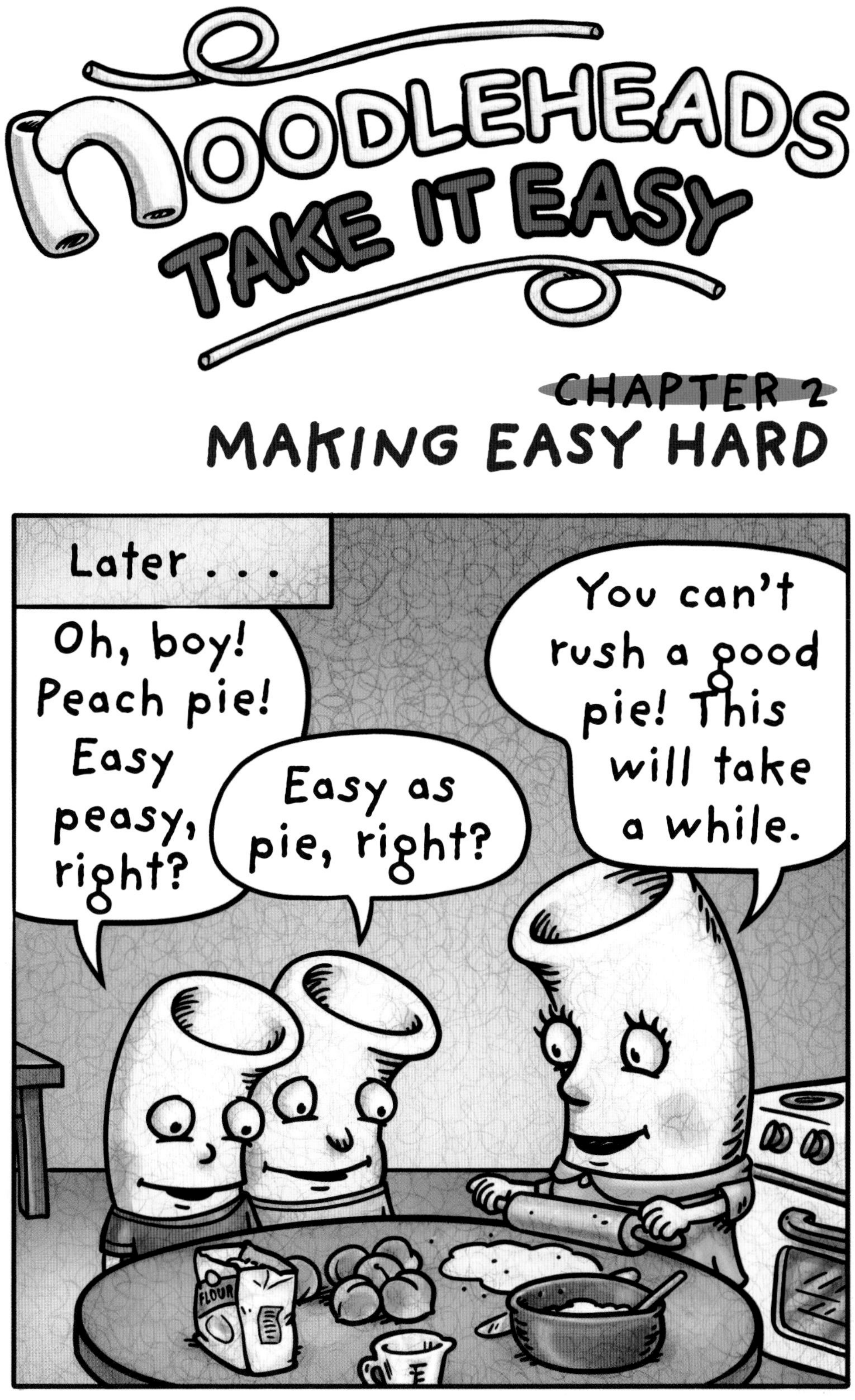
Later . . .
Oh, boy! Peach pie! Easy peasy, right?
Easy as pie, right?
You can't rush a good pie! This will take a while.
FLOUR

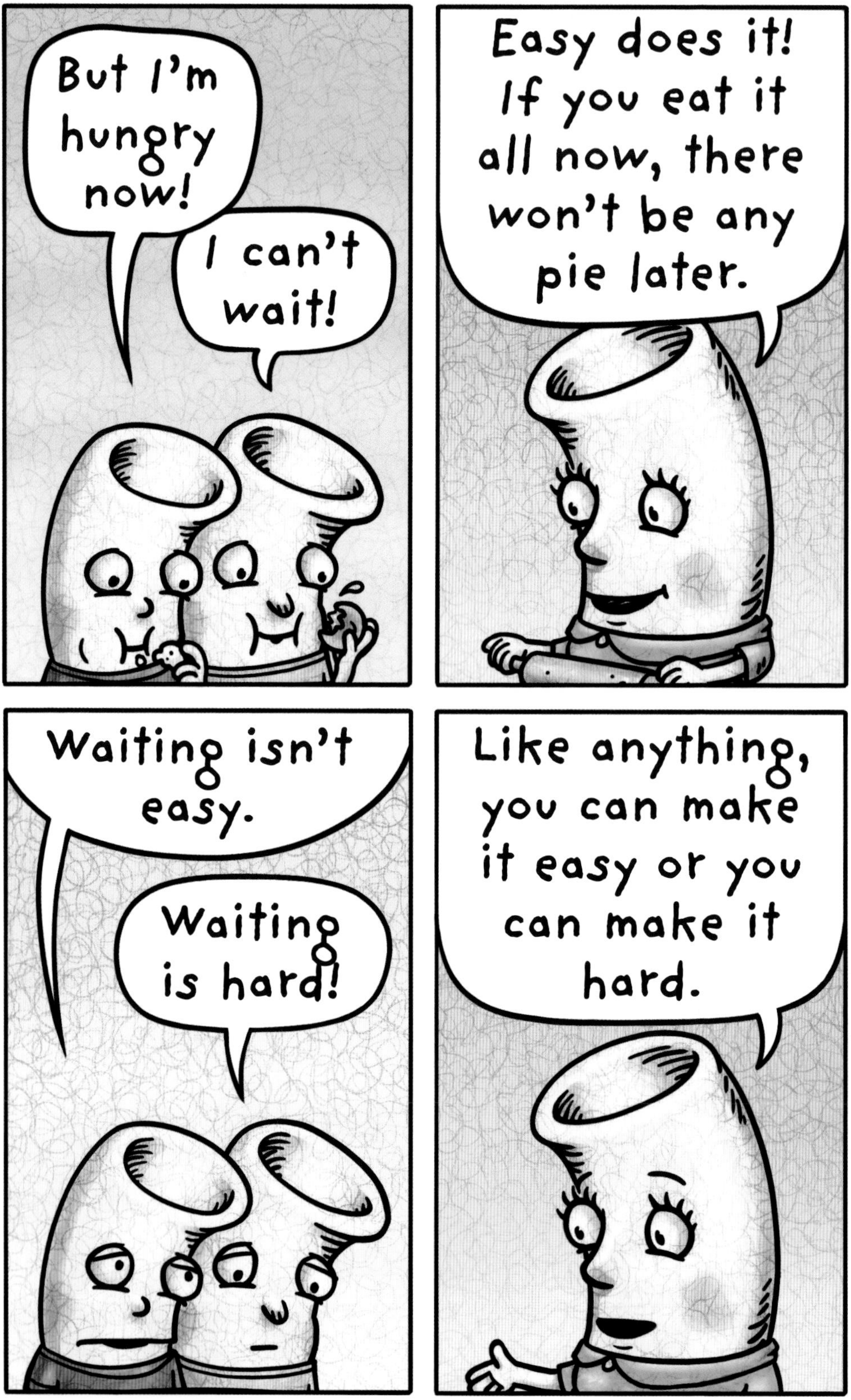
But I'm hungry now!
I can't wait!
Easy does it! If you eat it all now, there won't be any pie later.
Waiting isn't easy.
Waiting is hard!
Like anything, you can make it easy or you can make it hard.

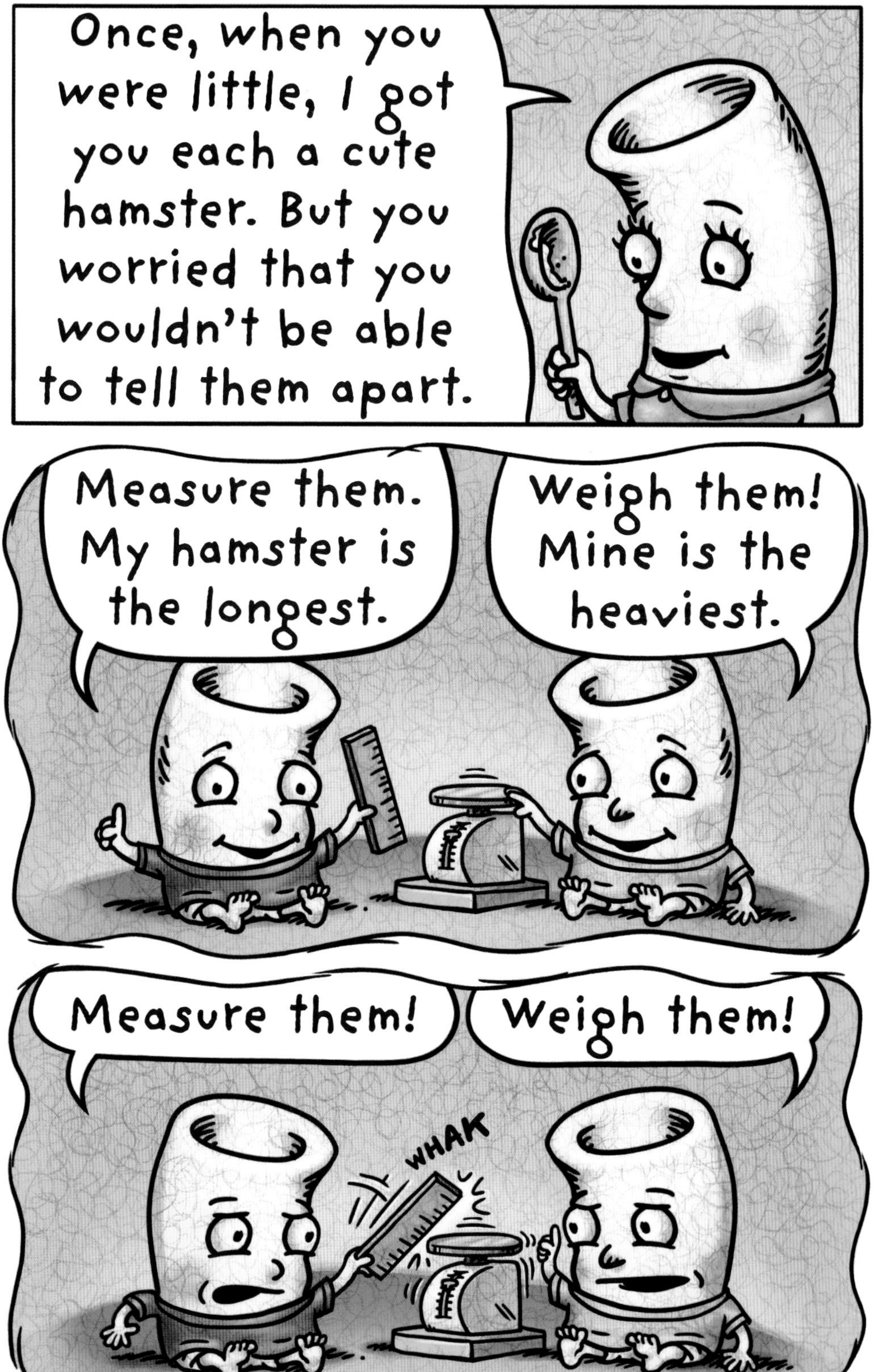

Once, when you were little, I got you each a cute hamster. But you worried that you wouldn't be able to tell them apart.
Measure them. My hamster is the longest.
Weigh them! Mine is the heaviest.
Measure them!
Weigh them!
WHAK

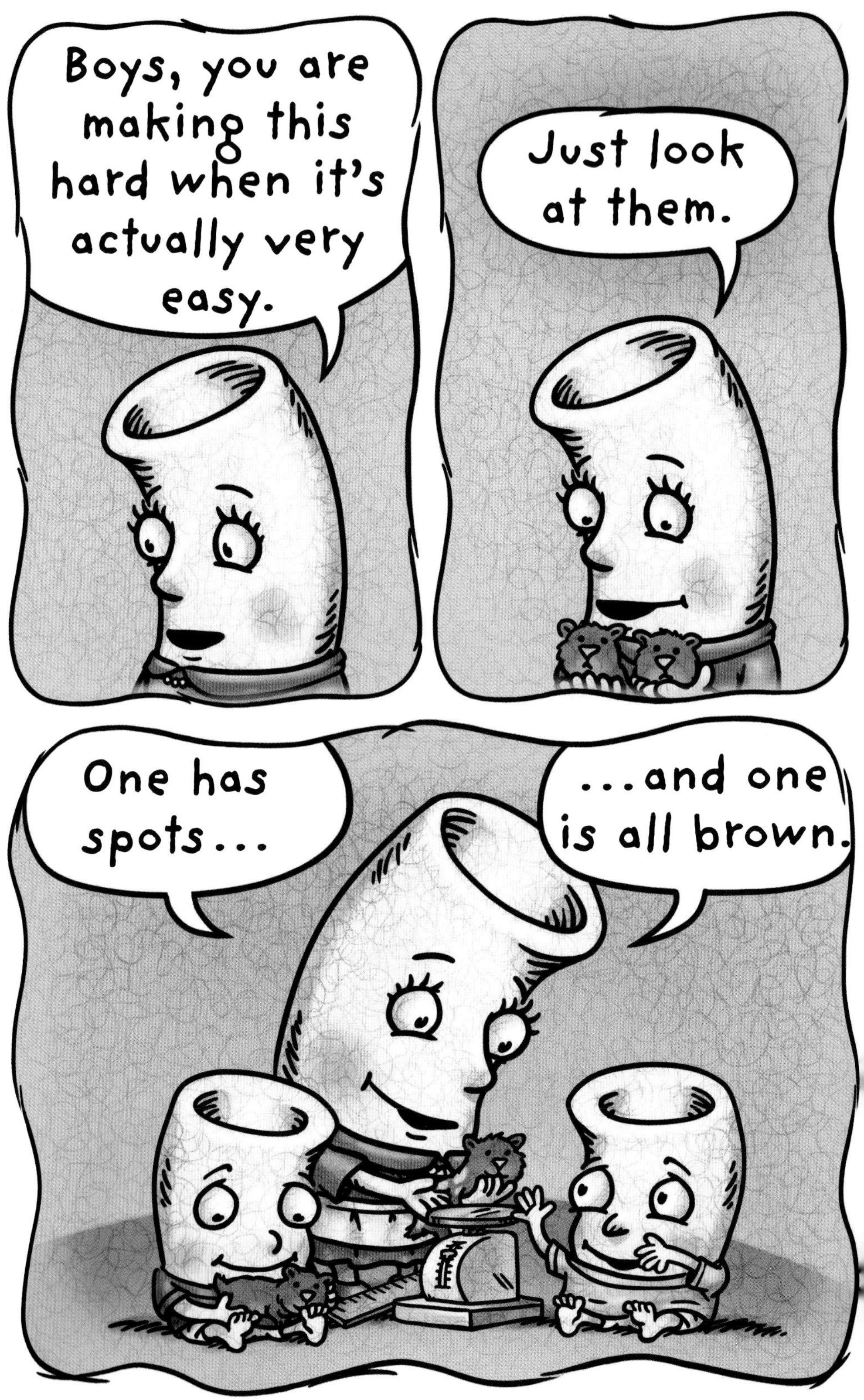
Boys, you are making this hard when it's actually very easy.
Just look at them.
One has spots...
...and one is all brown.

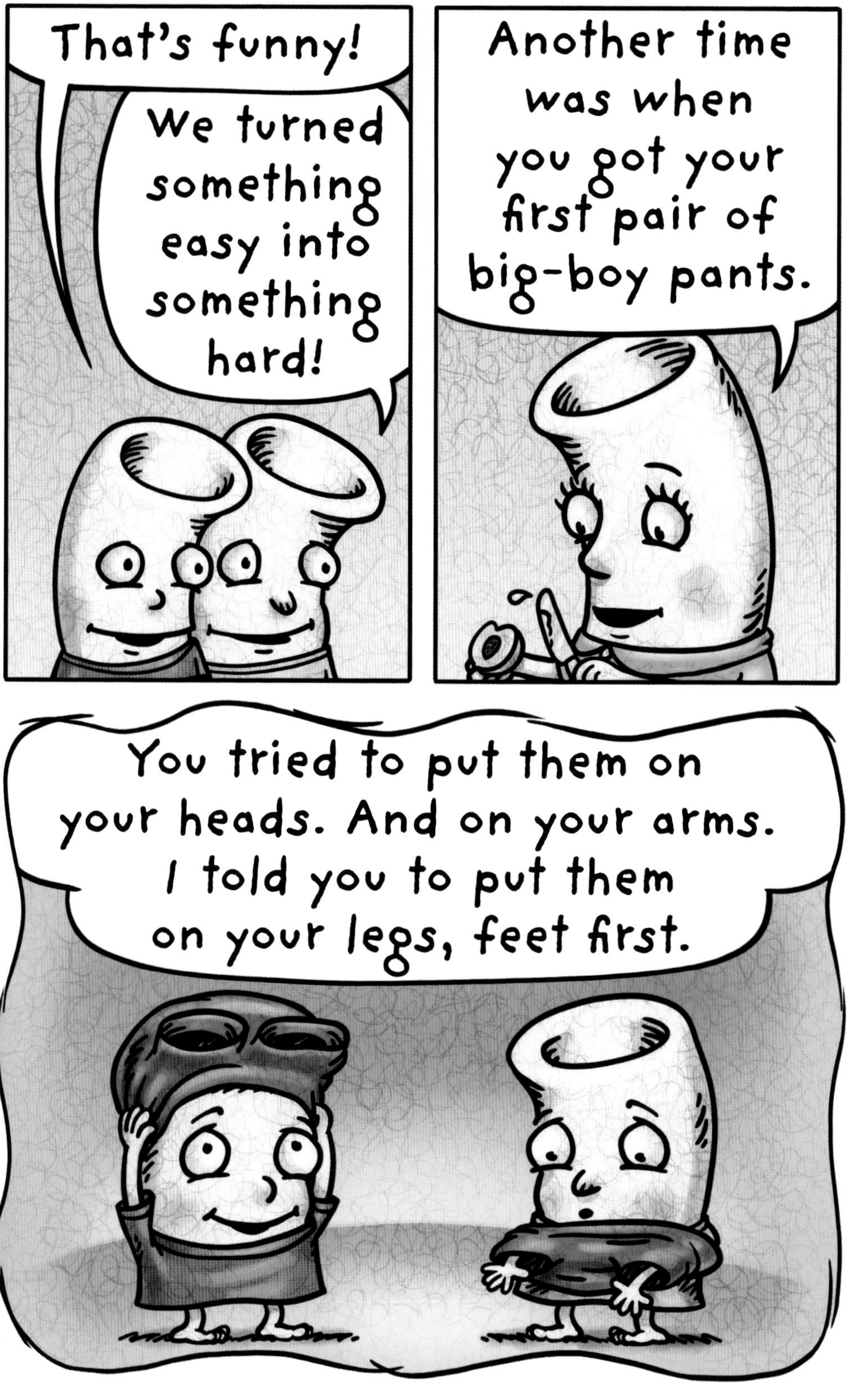
That's funny!
We turned something easy into something hard!
Another time was when you got your first pair of big-boy pants.
You tried to put them on your heads. And on your arms. I told you to put them on your legs, feet first.

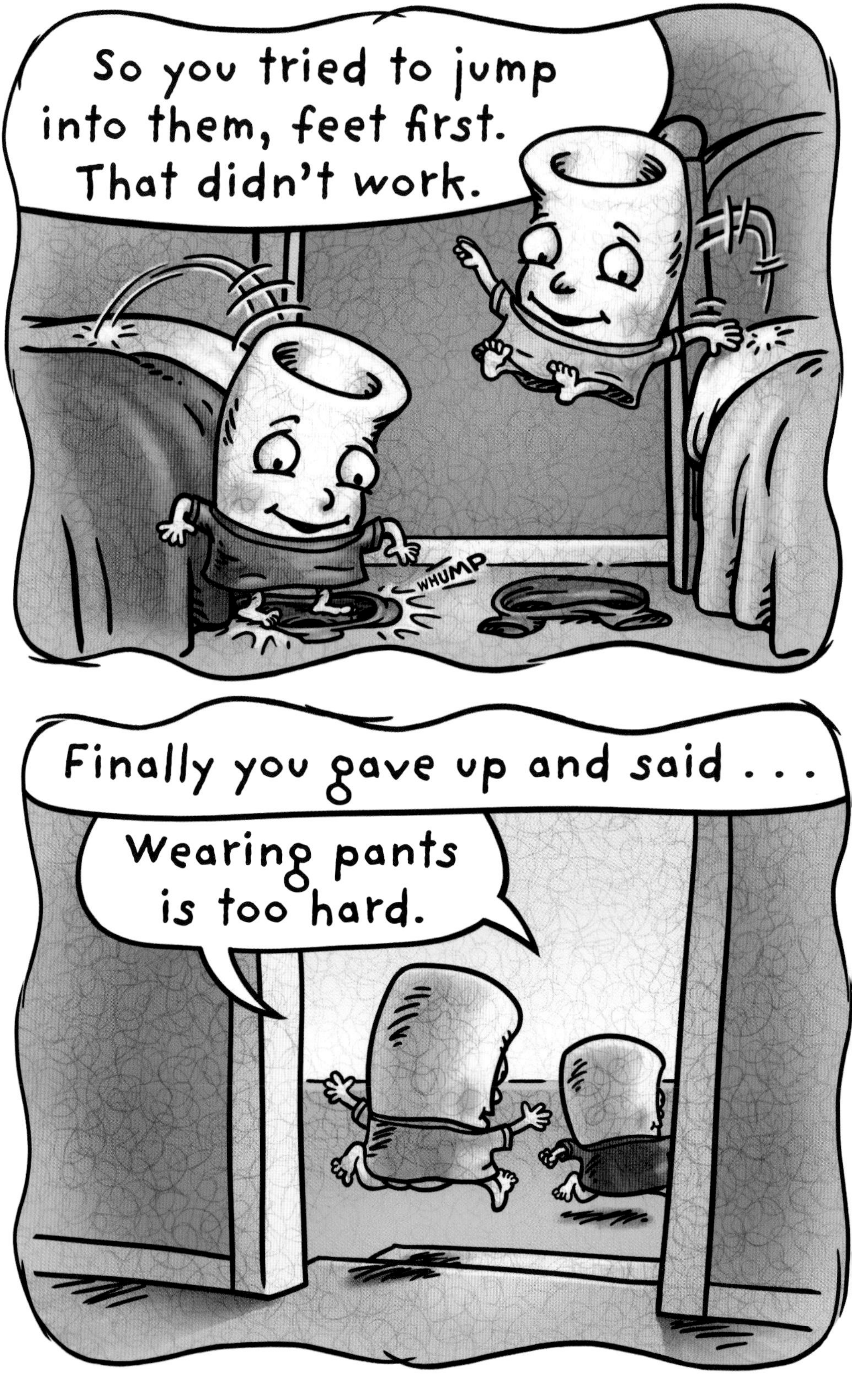
So you tried to jump into them, feet first. That didn't work.
WHUMP
Finally you gave up and said . . .
Wearing pants is too hard.

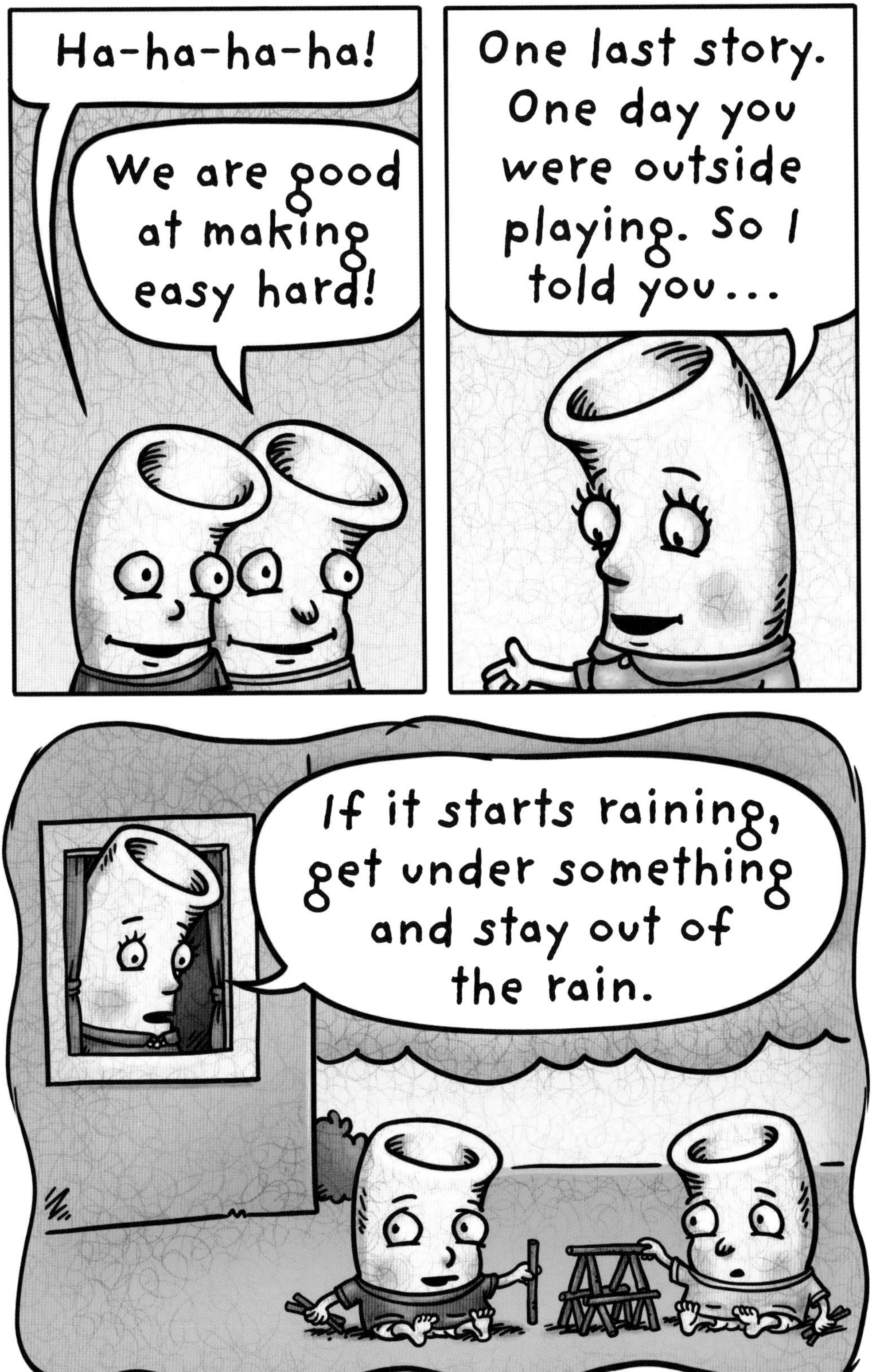
Ha-ha-ha-ha!
We are good at making easy hard!
One last story. One day you were outside playing. So I told you...
If it starts raining, get under something and stay out of the rain.

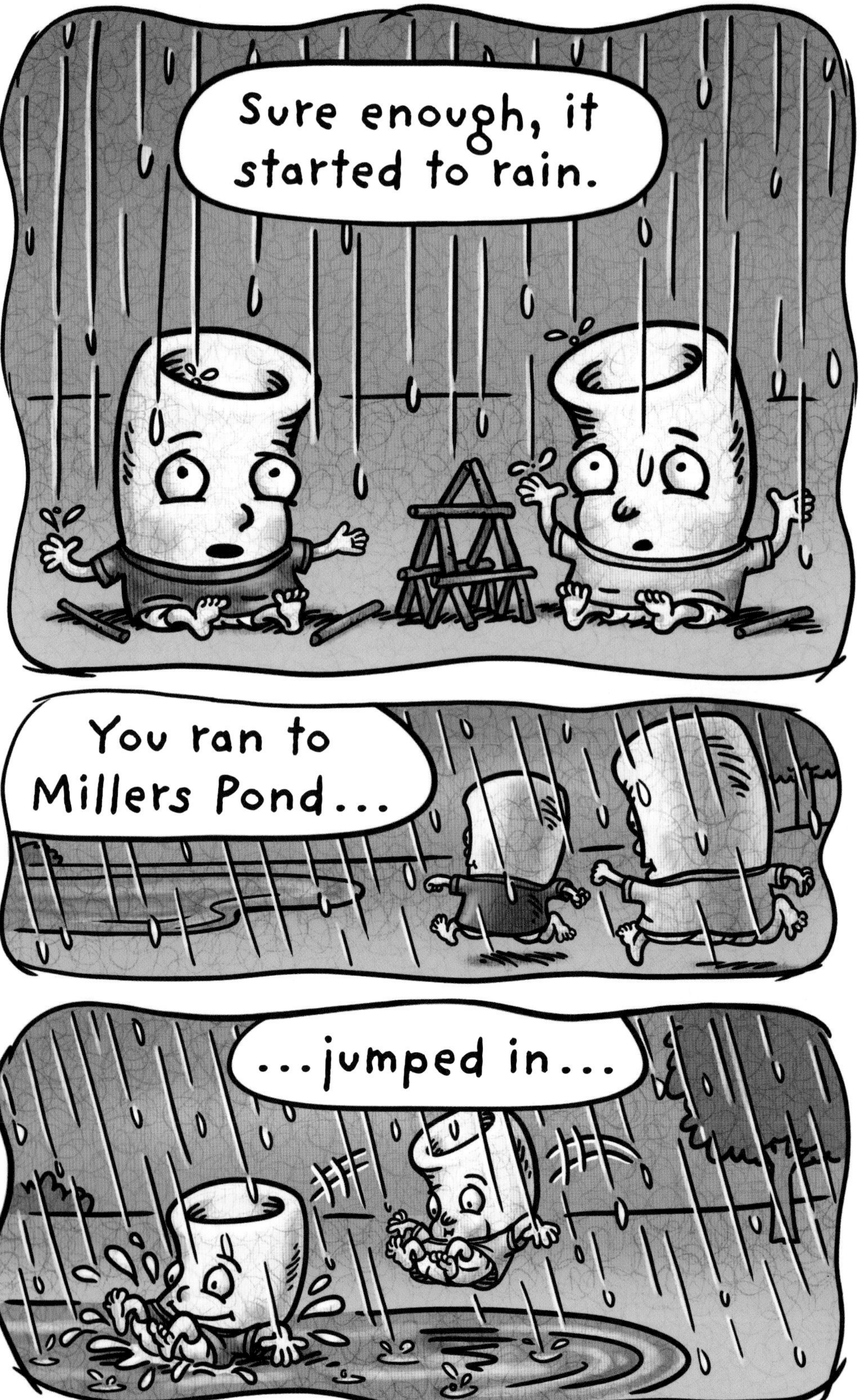
Sure enough, it started to rain.
You ran to Millers Pond...
...jumped in...

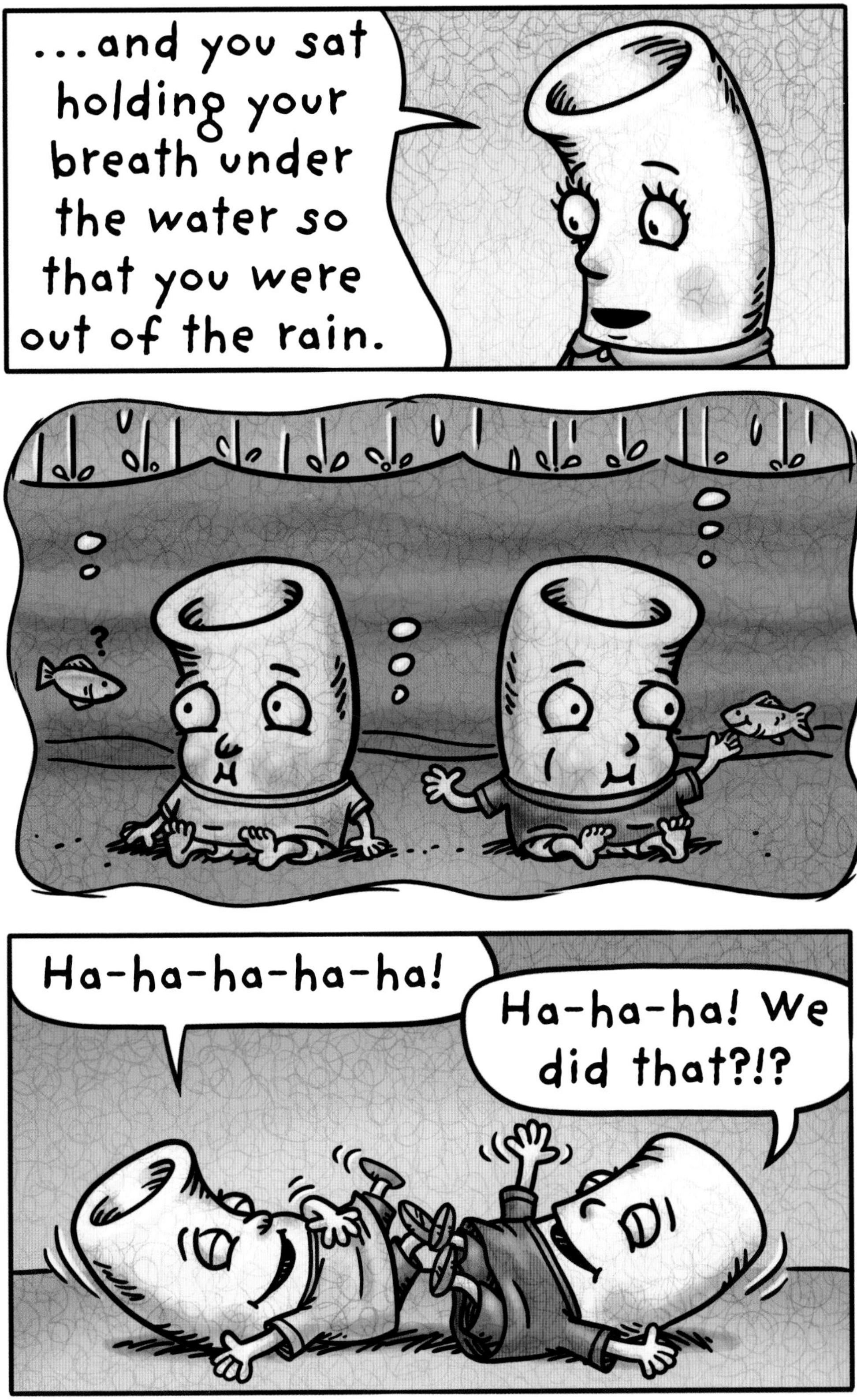
...and you sat holding your breath under the water so that you were out of the rain.
Ha-ha-ha-ha-ha!
Ha-ha-ha! We did that?!?

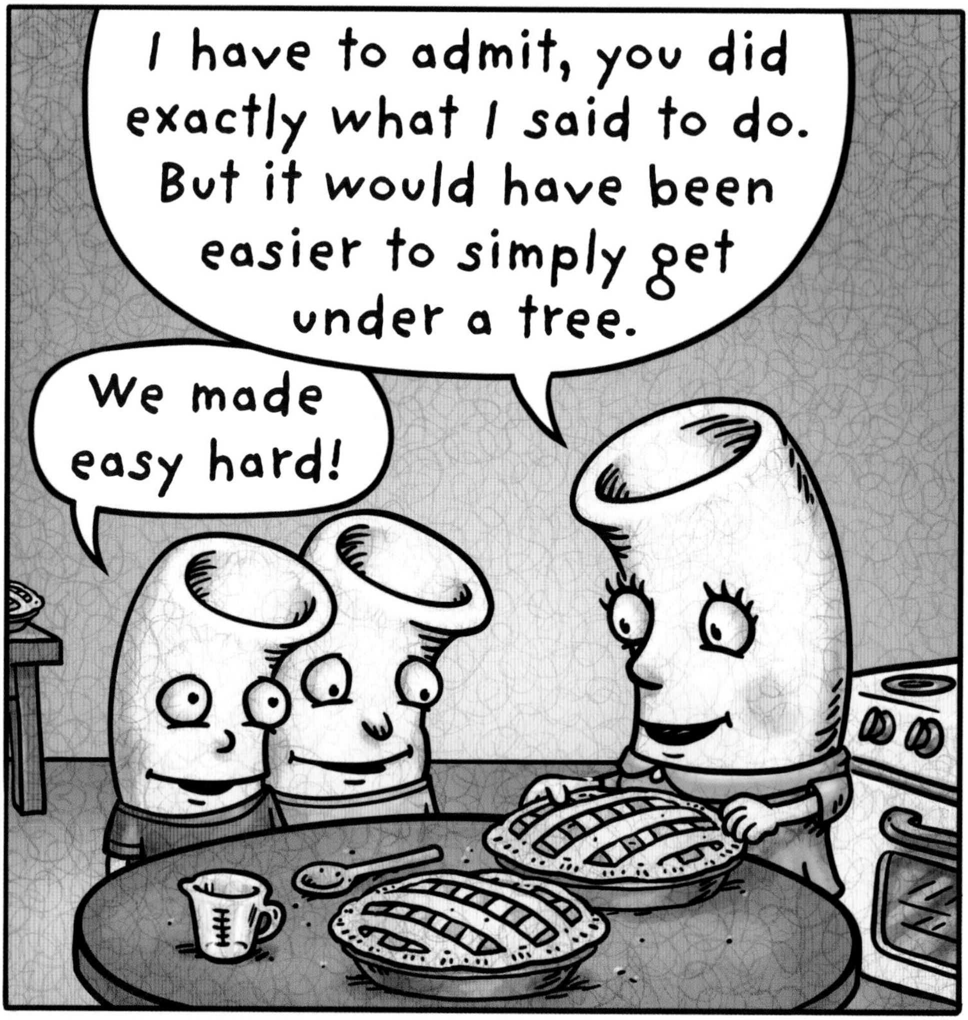
I have to admit, you did exactly what I said to do. But it would have been easier to simply get under a tree.
We made easy hard!

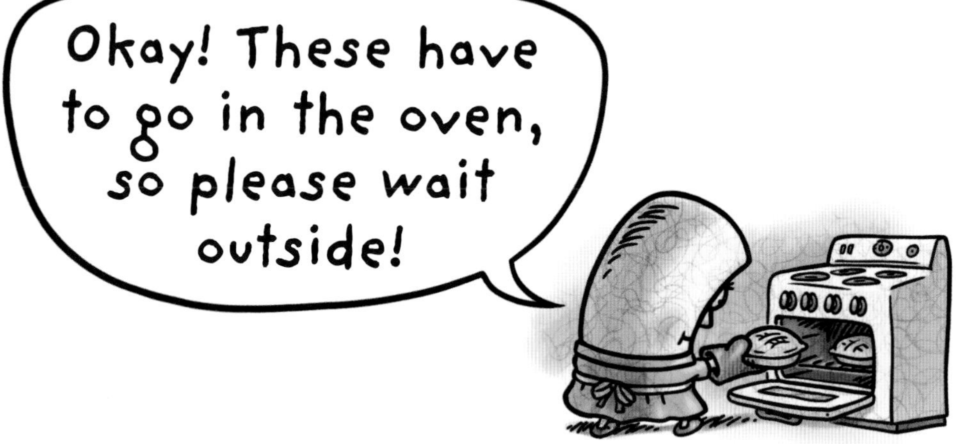
Okay! These have to go in the oven, so please wait outside!

NOODLEHEADS TAKE IT EASY

CHAPTER 3
EASY COME, EASY GO

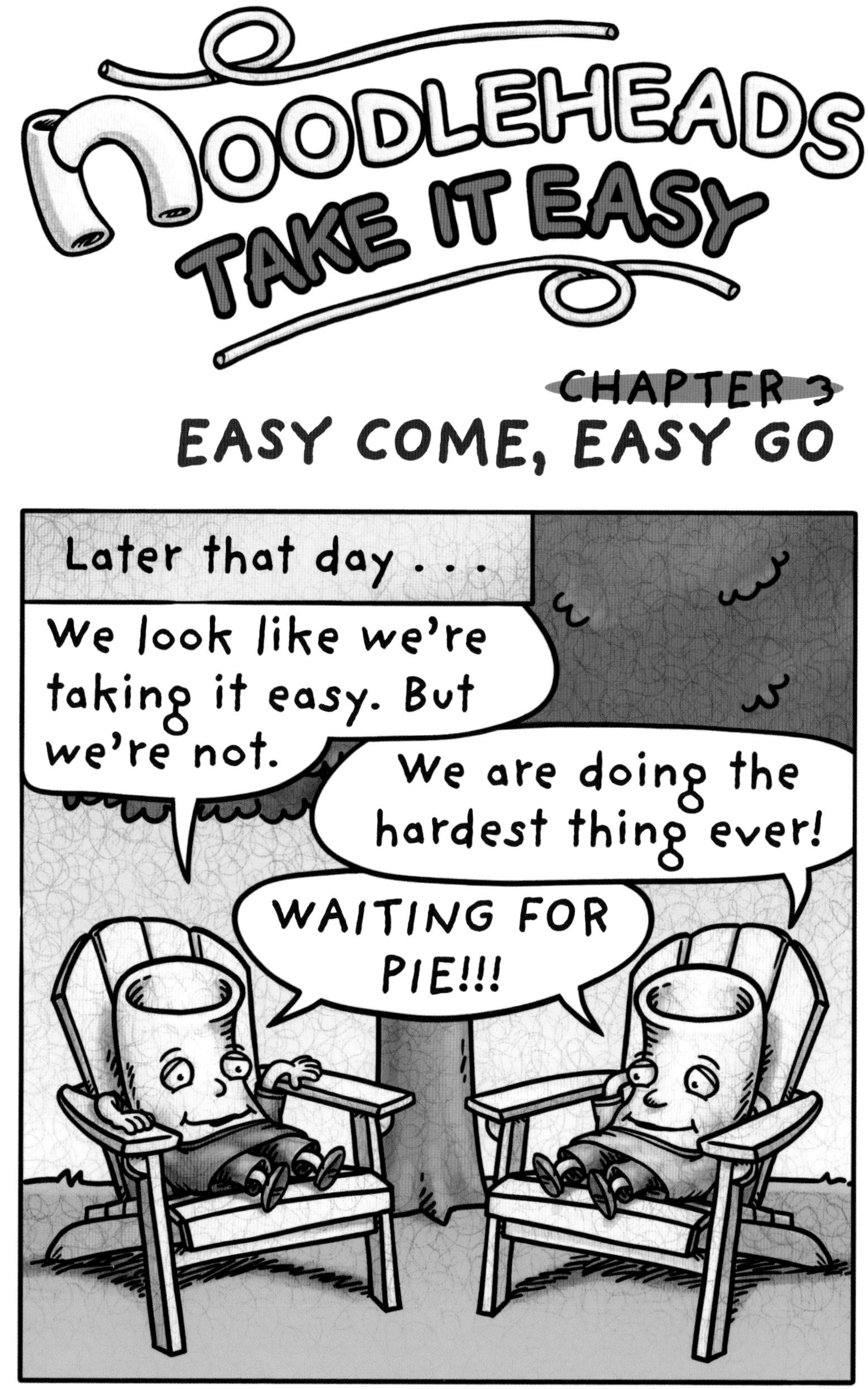
Later that day . . .
We look like we're taking it easy. But we're not.
We are doing the hardest thing ever!
WAITING FOR PIE!!!

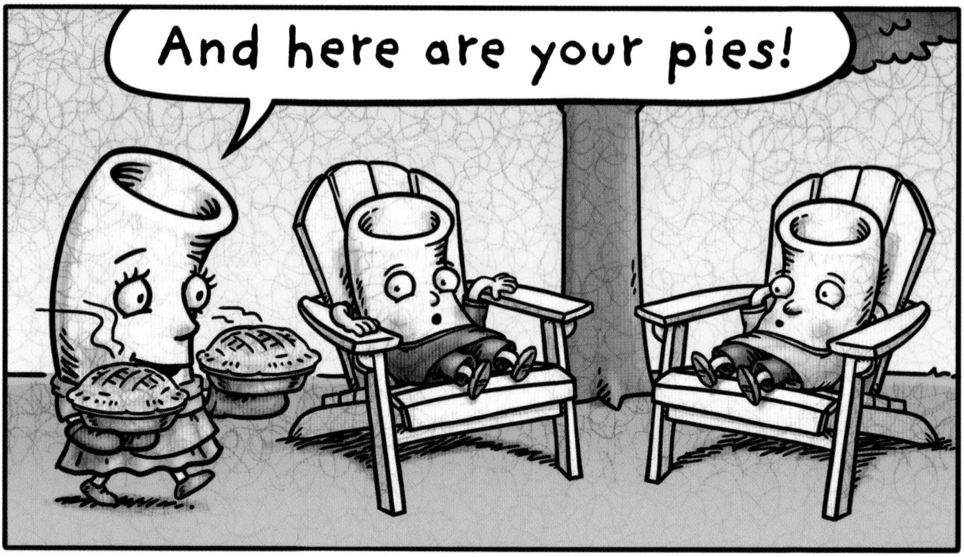
And here are your pies!

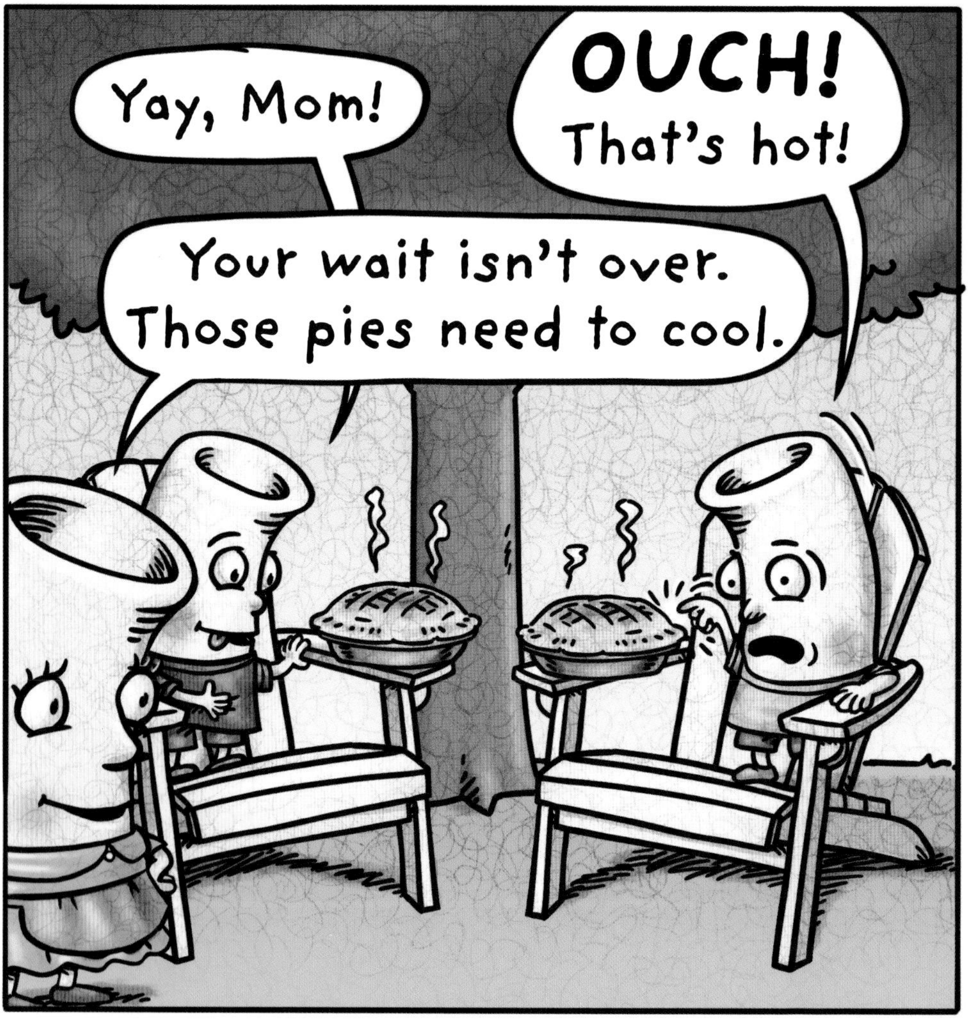
Yay, Mom!
OUCH! That's hot!
Your wait isn't over. Those pies need to cool.

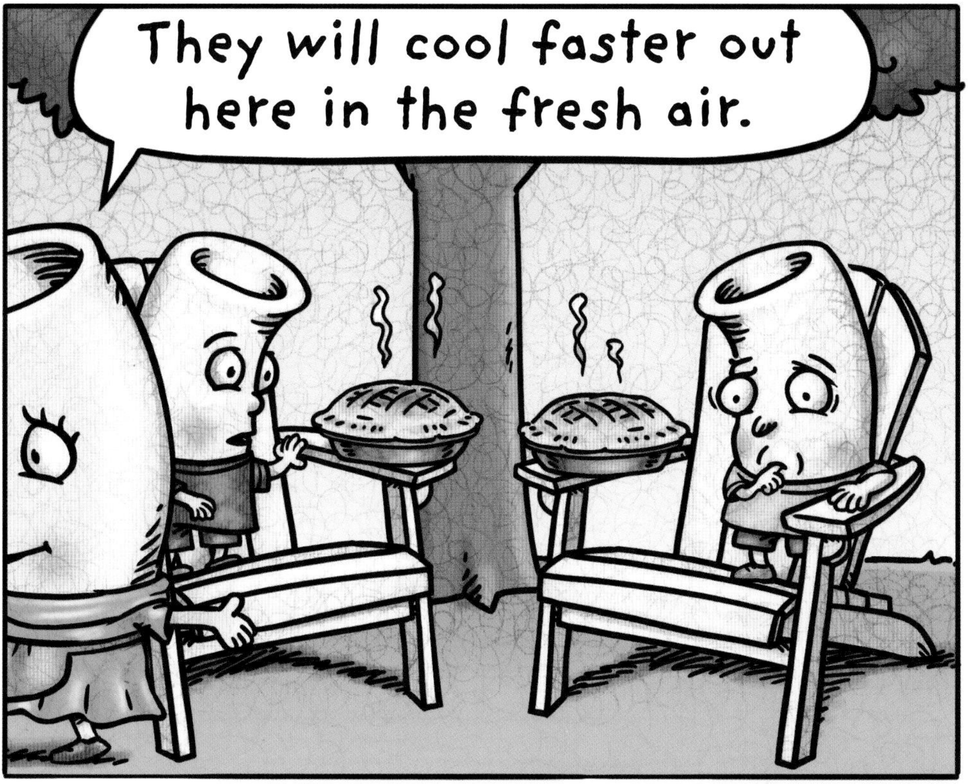
They will cool faster out here in the fresh air.

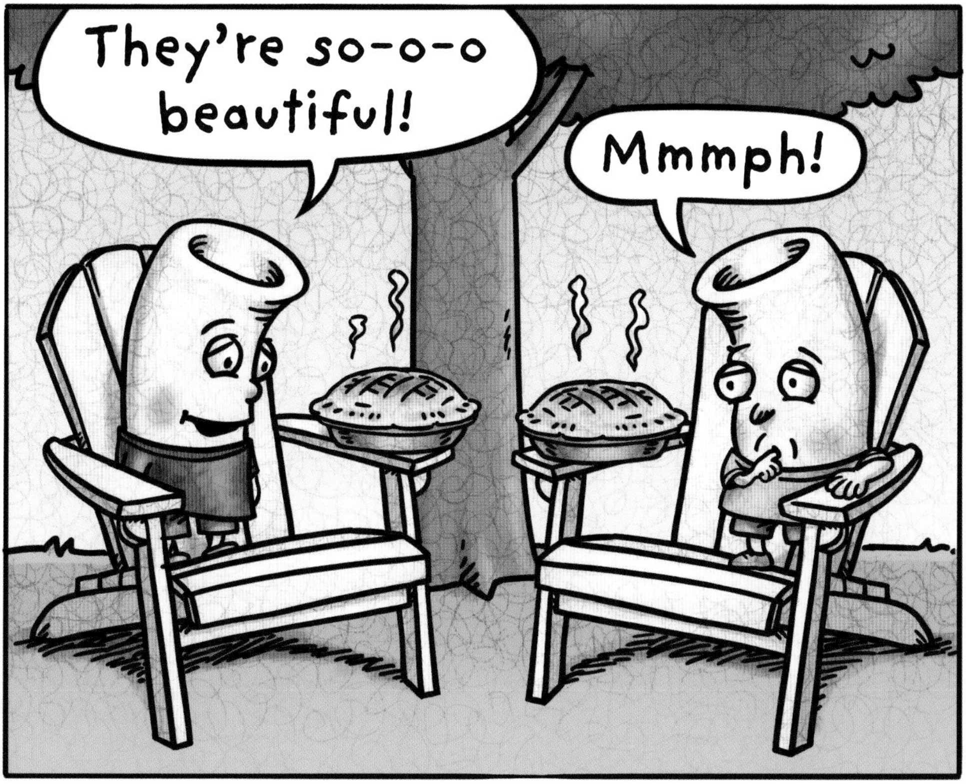
They're so-o-o beautiful!
Mmmph!

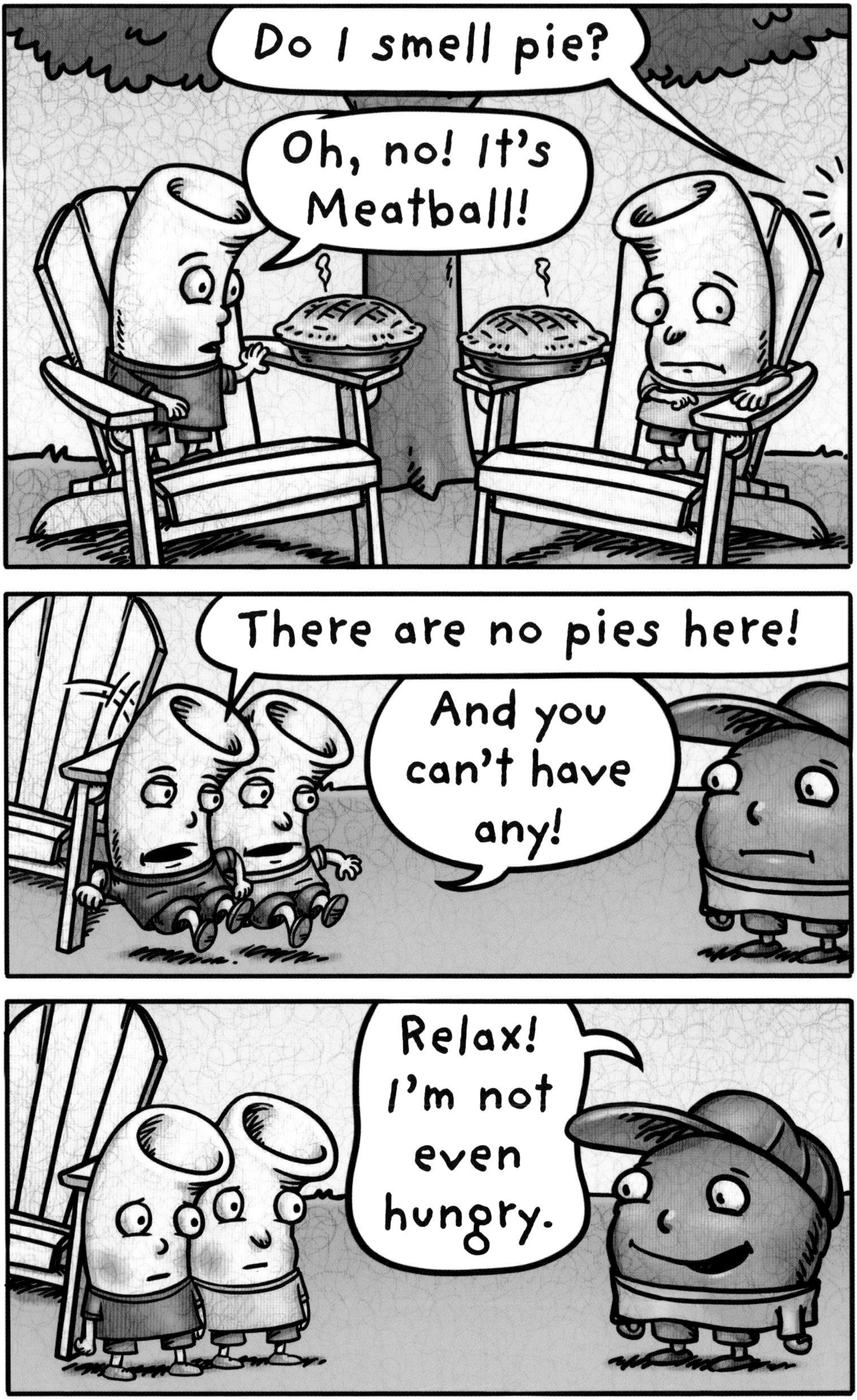
Do I smell pie?
Oh, no! It's Meatball!
There are no pies here!
And you can't have any!
Relax! I'm not even hungry.

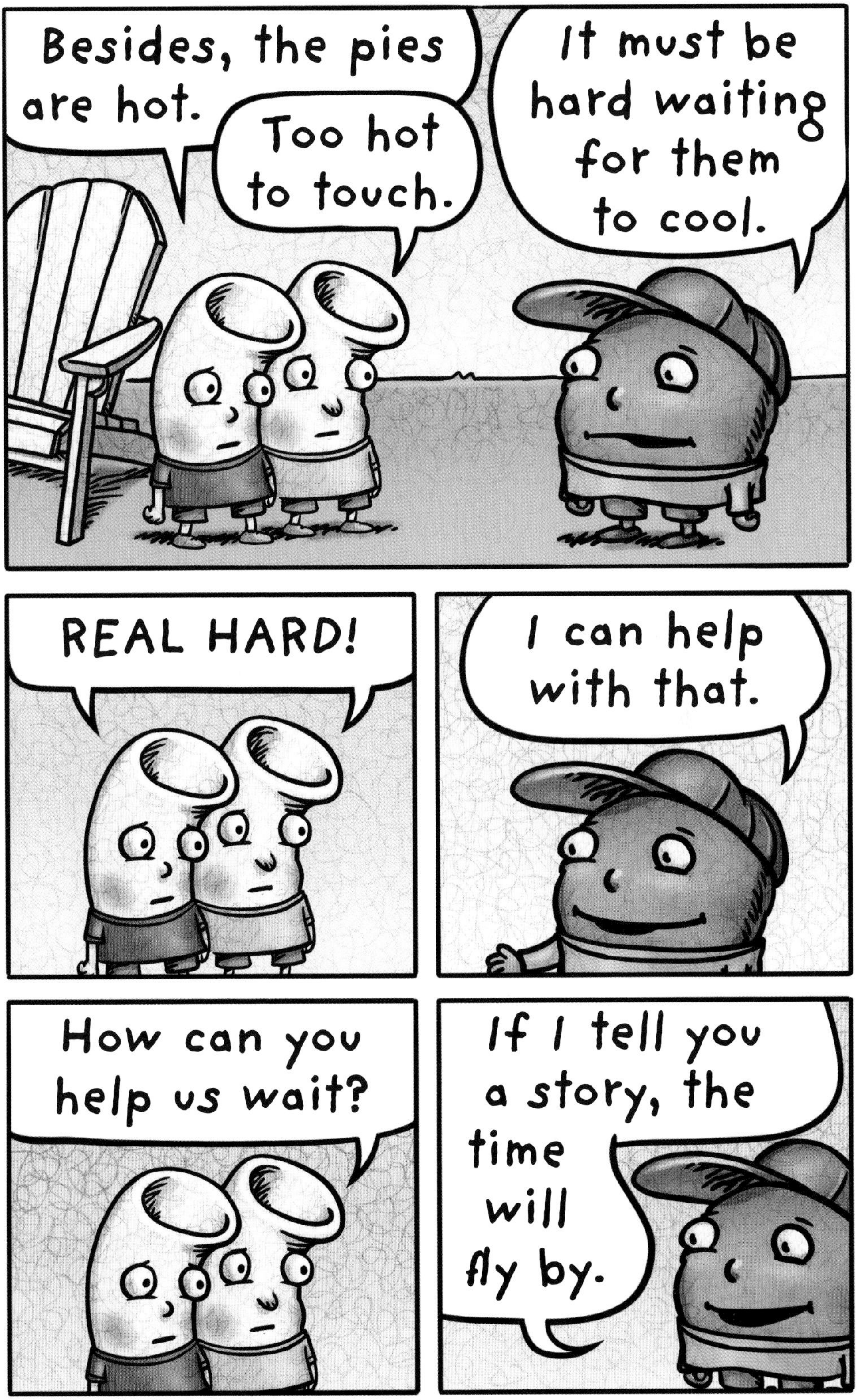
Besides, the pies are hot.
Too hot to touch.
It must be hard waiting for them to cool.
REAL HARD!
I can help with that.
How can you help us wait?
If I tell you a story, the time will fly by.

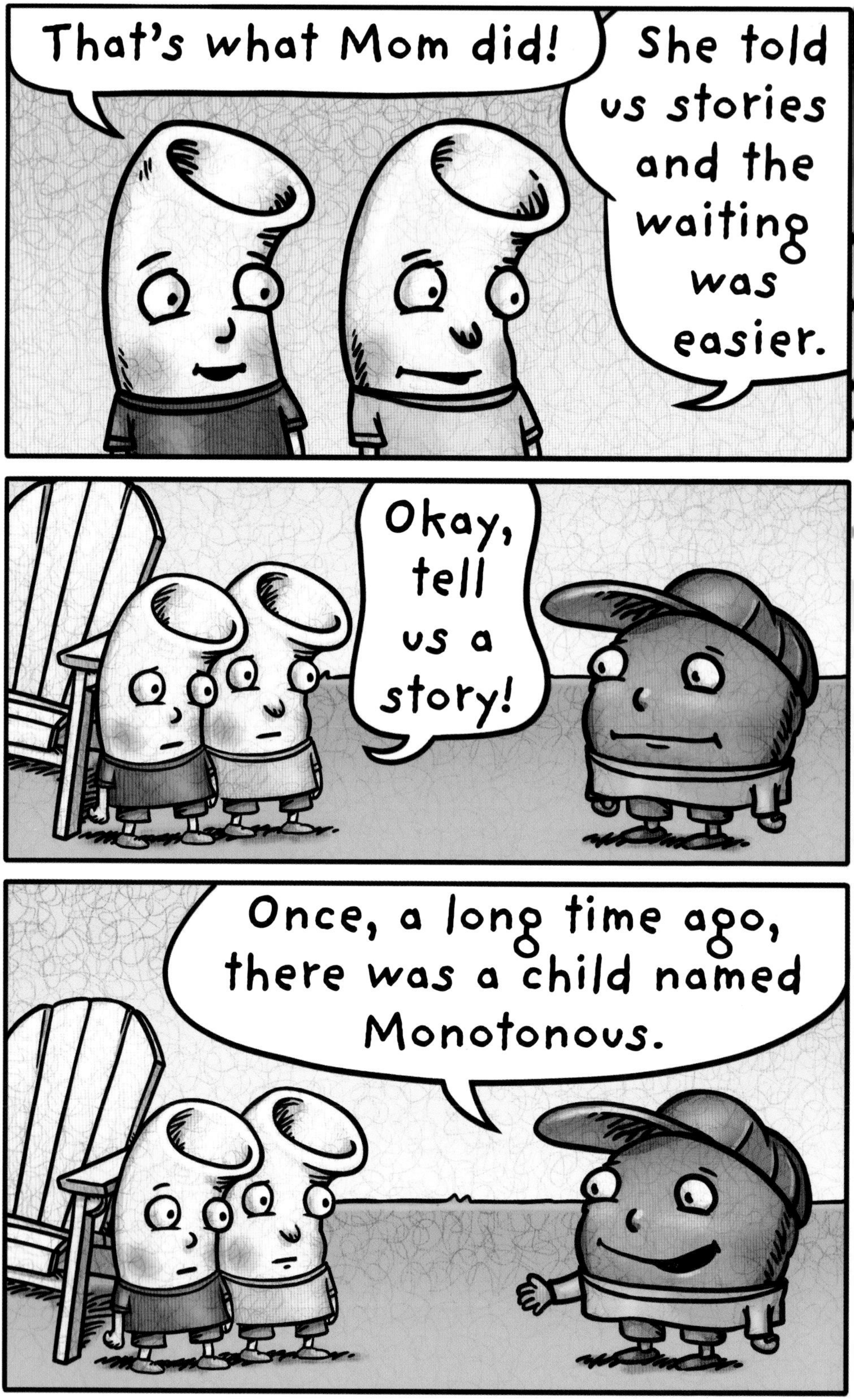
That's what Mom did!
She told us stories and the waiting was easier.
Okay, tell us a story!
Once, a long time ago, there was a child named Monotonous.

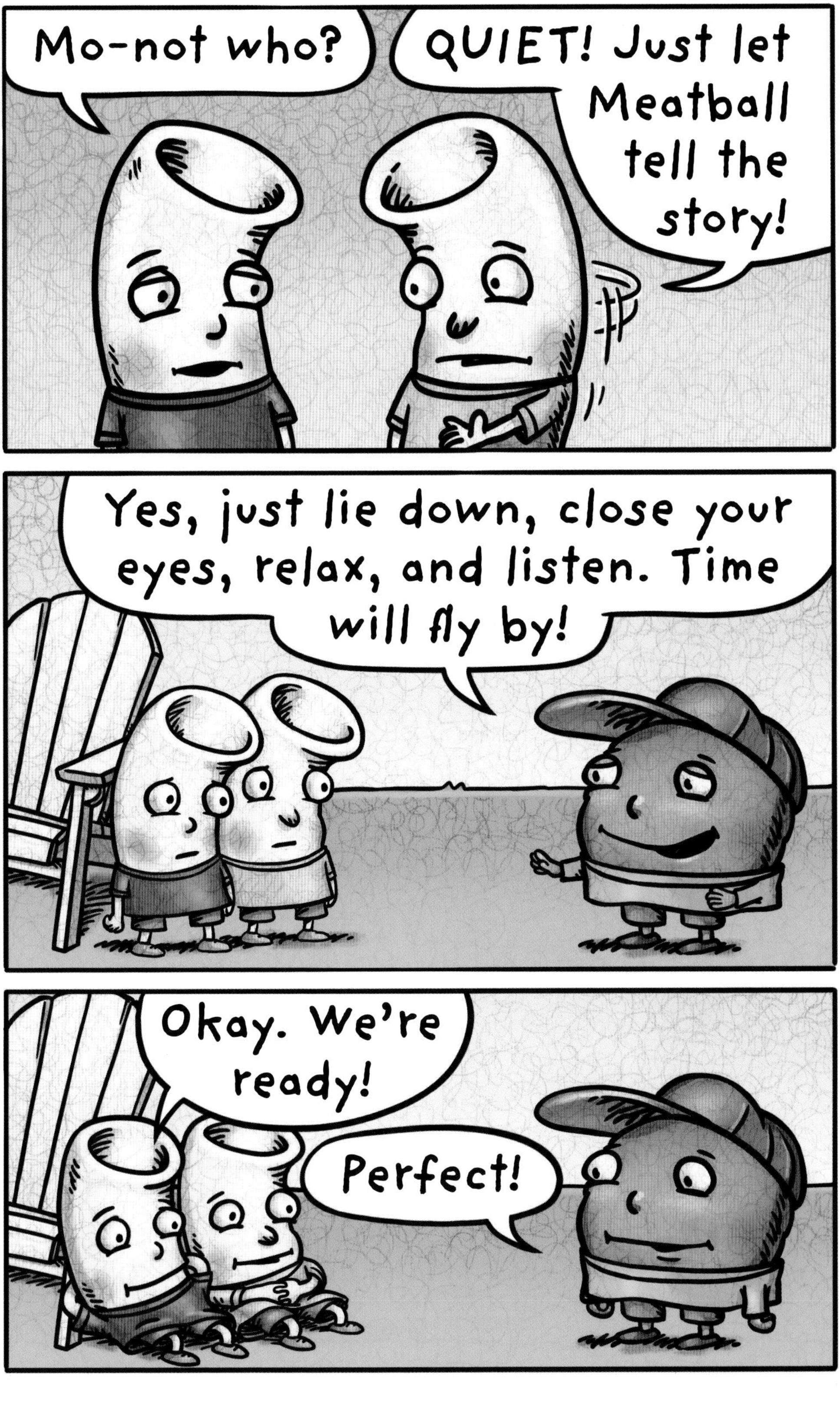
Mo-not who?
QUIET! Just let Meatball tell the story!
Yes, just lie down, close your eyes, relax, and listen. Time will fly by!
Okay. We're ready!
Perfect!

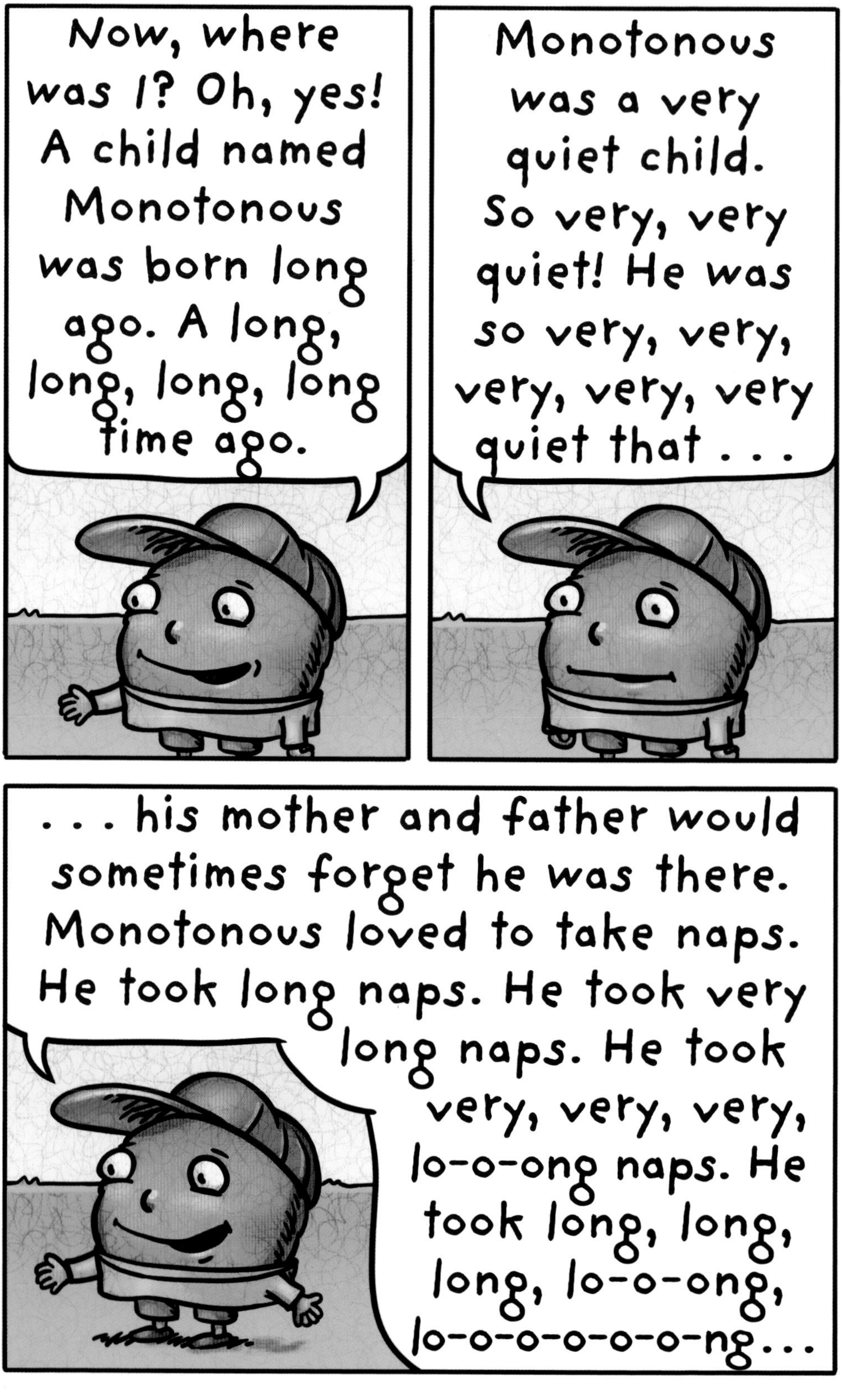
Now, where was I? Oh, yes! A child named Monotonous was born long ago. A long, long, long, long time ago.
Monotonous was a very quiet child. So very, very quiet! He was so very, very, very, very, very quiet that . . .
. . . his mother and father would sometimes forget he was there. Monotonous loved to take naps. He took long naps. He took very long naps. He took very, very, very, lo-o-ong naps. He took long, long, long, lo-o-ong, lo-o-o-o-o-o-ng...

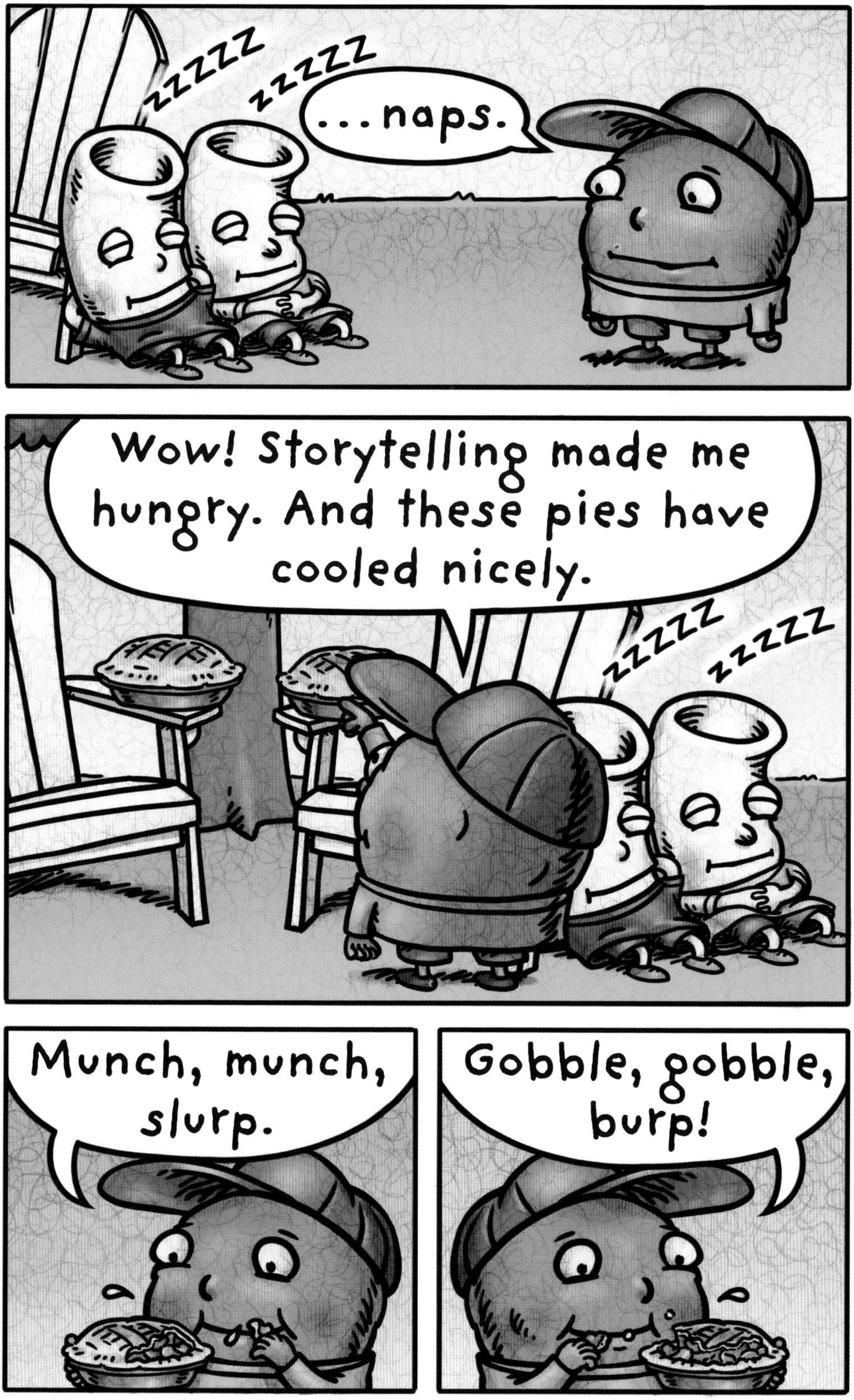
ZZZZZ
ZZZZZ
...naps.
Wow! Storytelling made me hungry. And these pies have cooled nicely.
ZZZZZ
ZZZZZ
Munch, munch, slurp.
Gobble, gobble, burp!

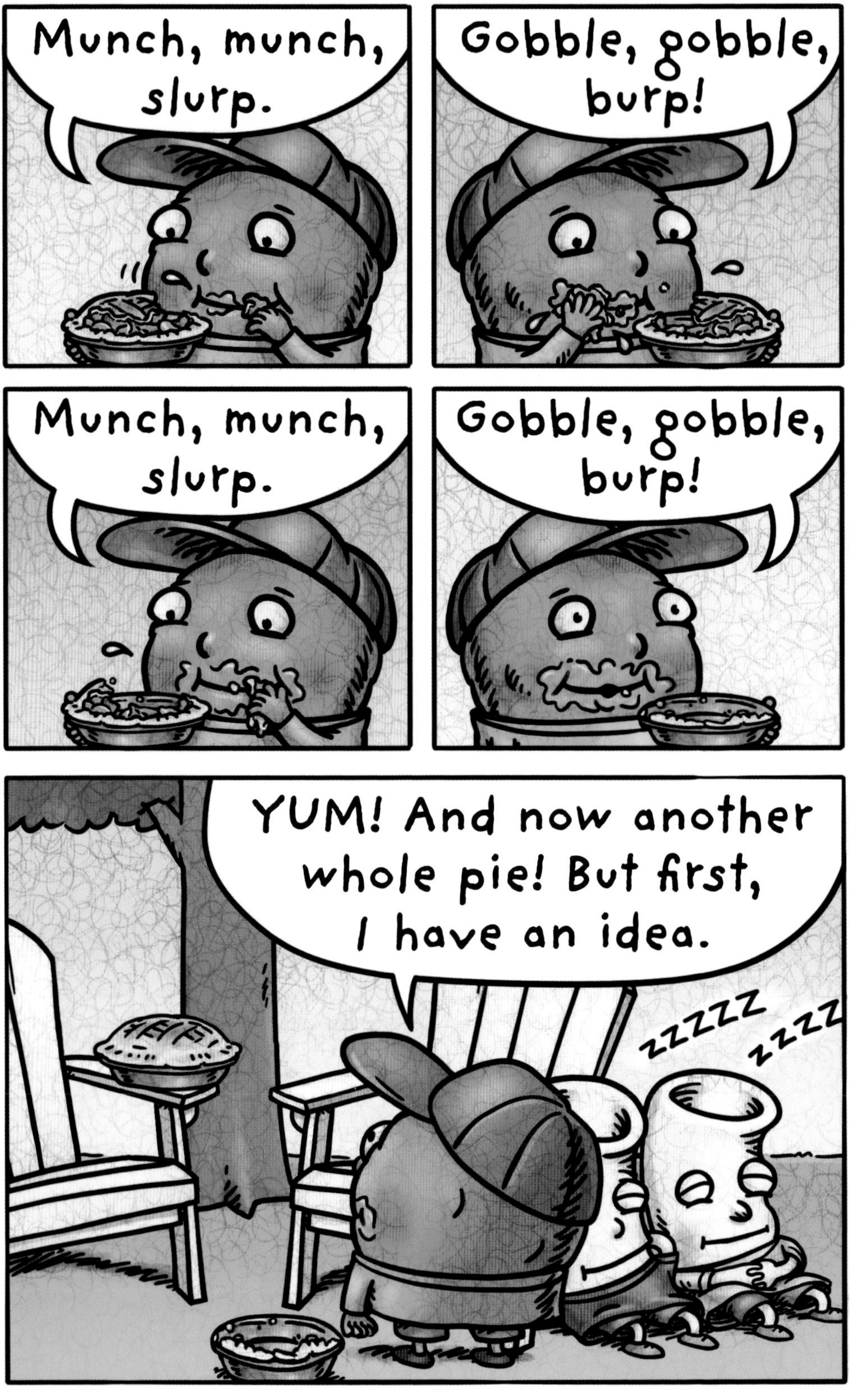
Munch, munch, slurp.
Gobble, gobble, burp!
Munch, munch, slurp.
Gobble, gobble, burp!
YUM! And now another whole pie! But first, I have an idea.
zzzzz
zzzz

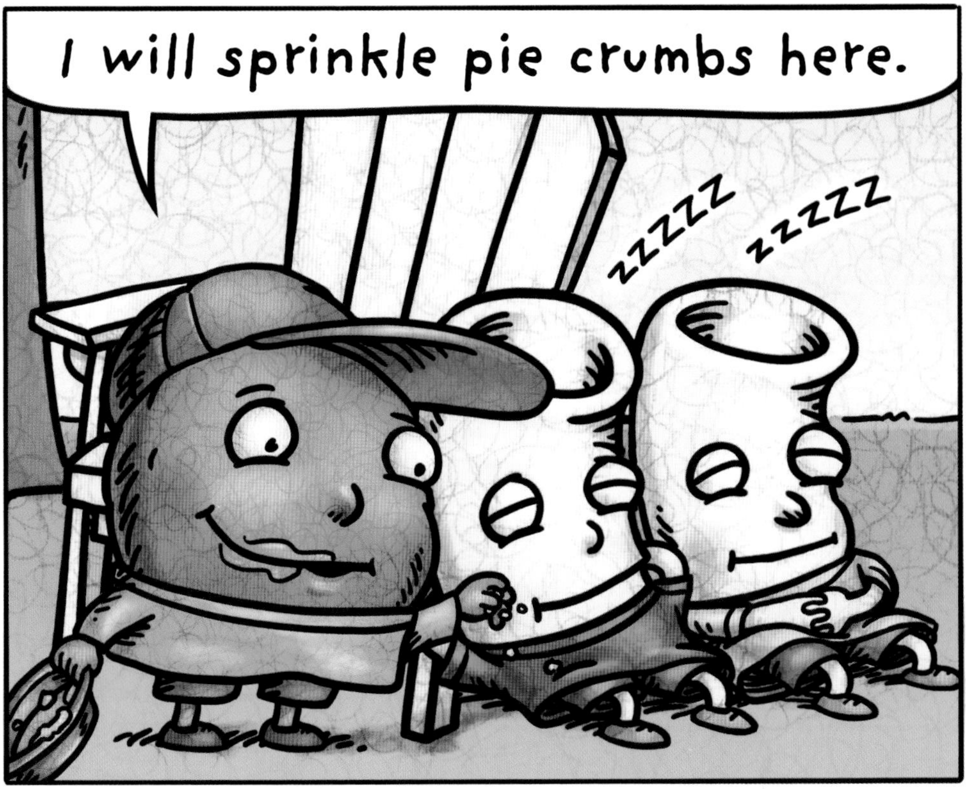
I will sprinkle pie crumbs here.
zzzzz
zzzzz

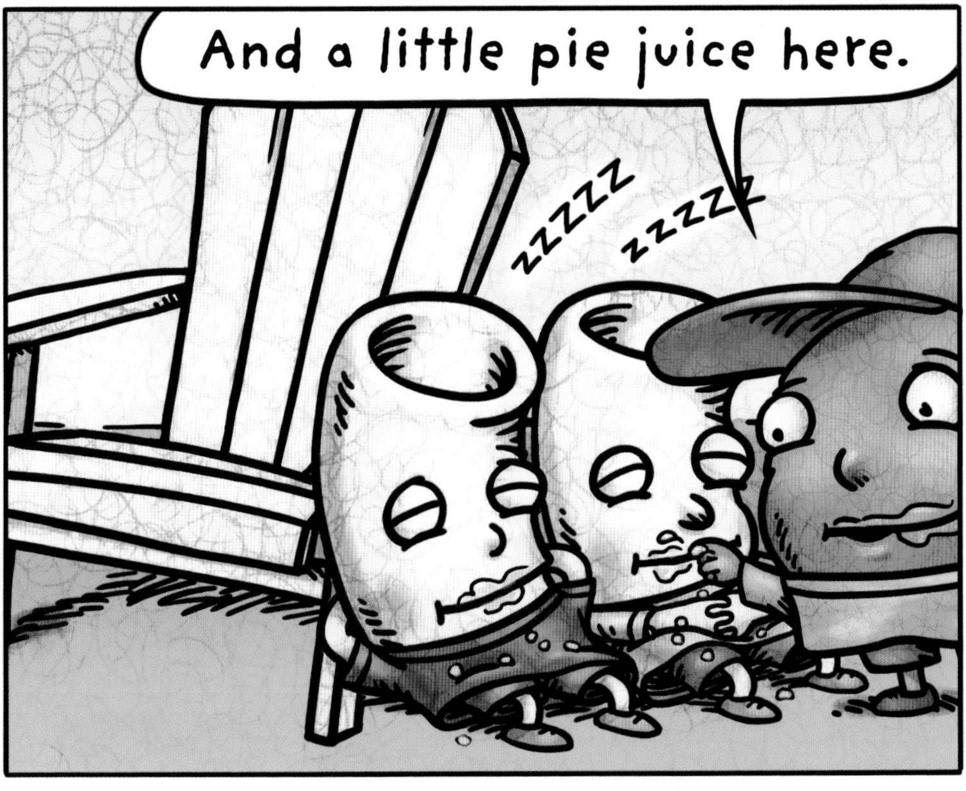
And a little pie juice here.
zzzzz
zzzzz

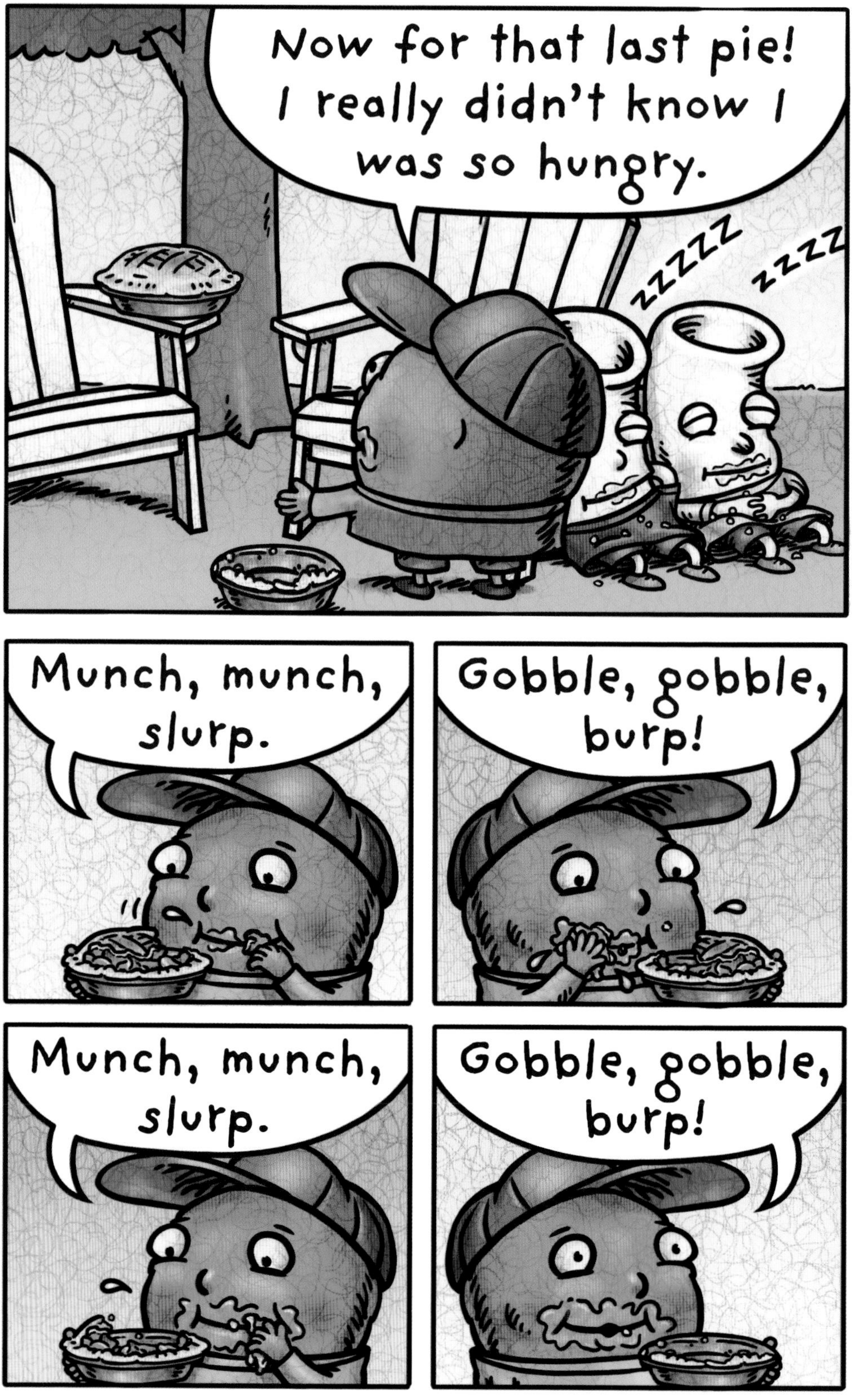
Now for that last pie! I really didn't know I was so hungry.
ZZZZZ
ZZZZ
Munch, munch, slurp.
Gobble, gobble, burp!
Munch, munch, slurp.
Gobble, gobble, burp!

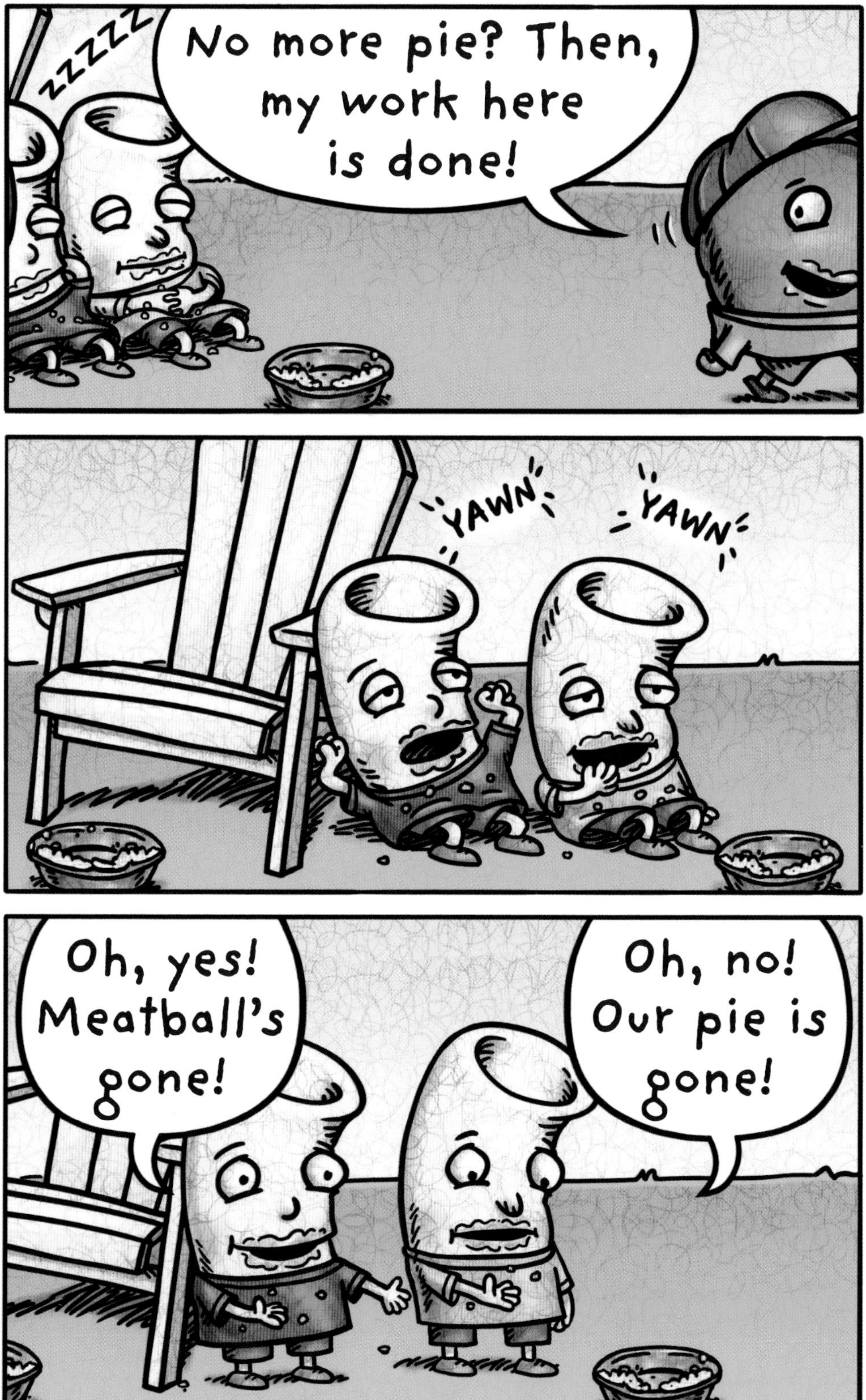
ZZZZZ
No more pie? Then, my work here is done!
YAWN
YAWN
Oh, yes! Meatball's gone!
Oh, no! Our pie is gone!

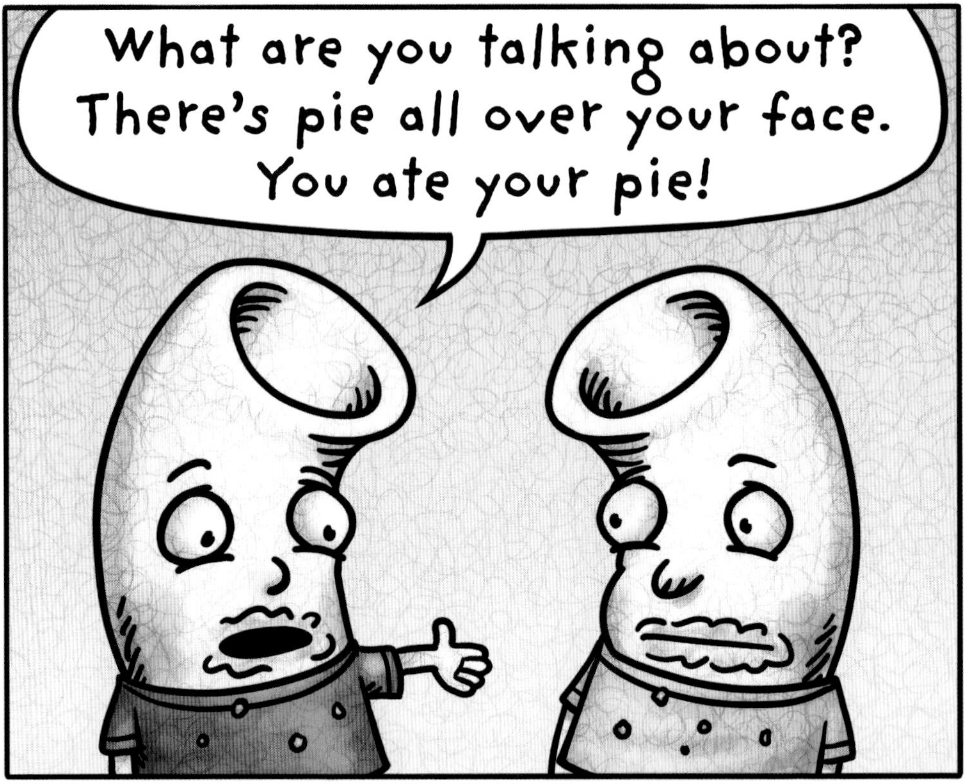
What are you talking about? There's pie all over your face. You ate your pie!

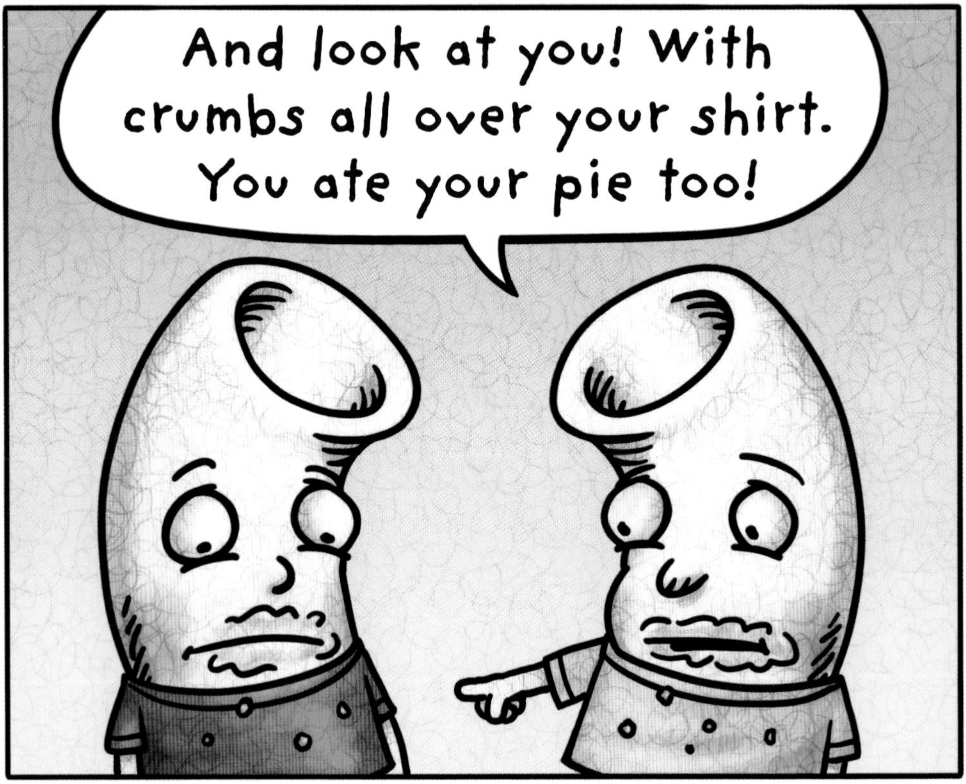
And look at you! With crumbs all over your shirt. You ate your pie too!

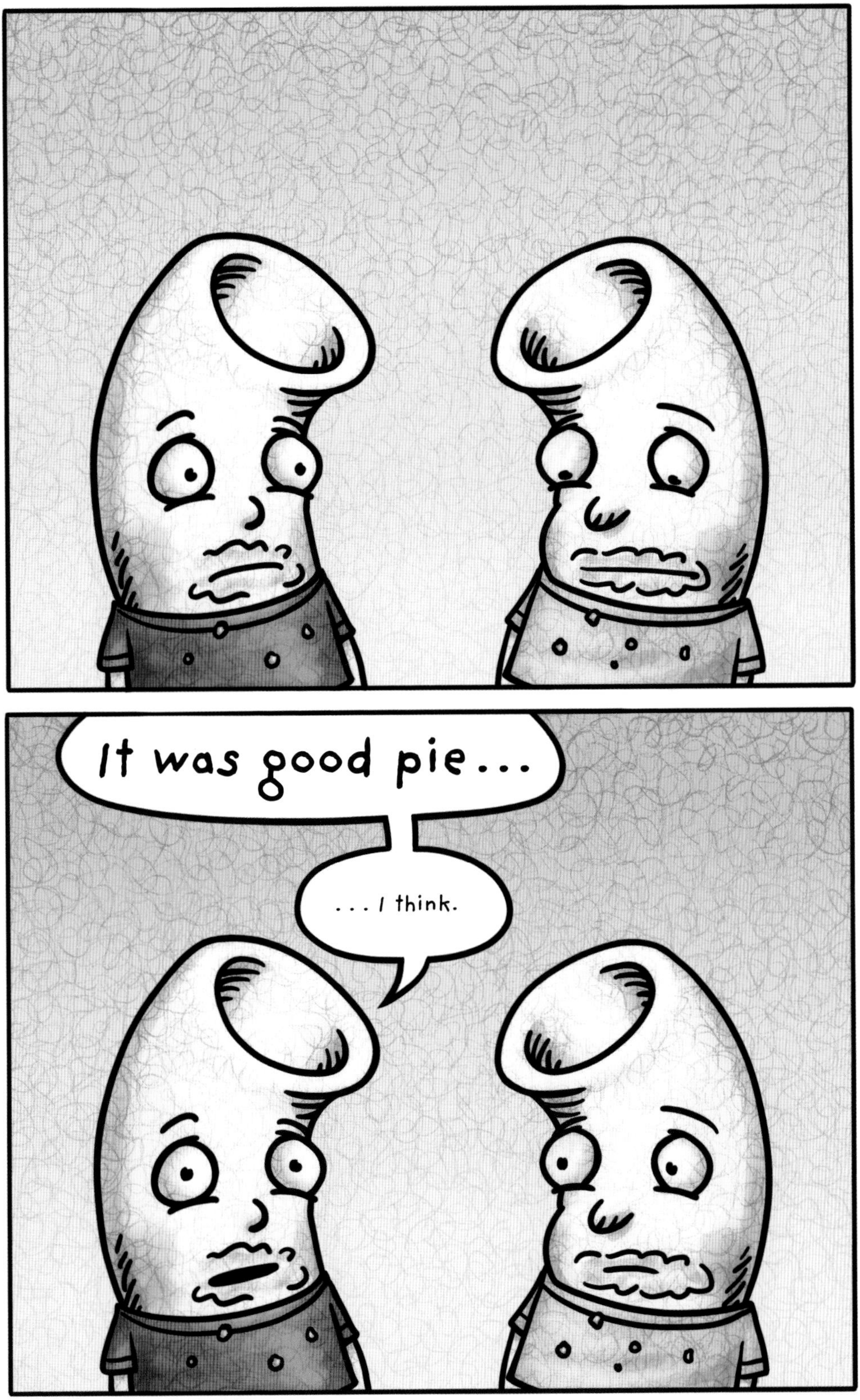
It was good pie...
. . . I think.

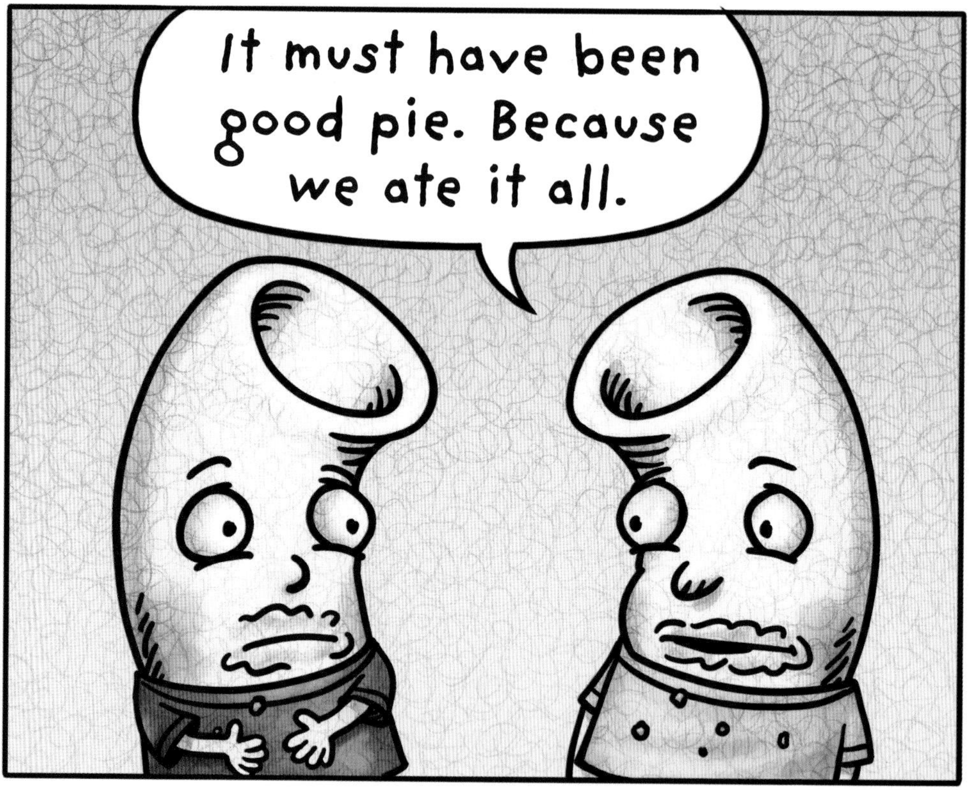
It must have been good pie. Because we ate it all.

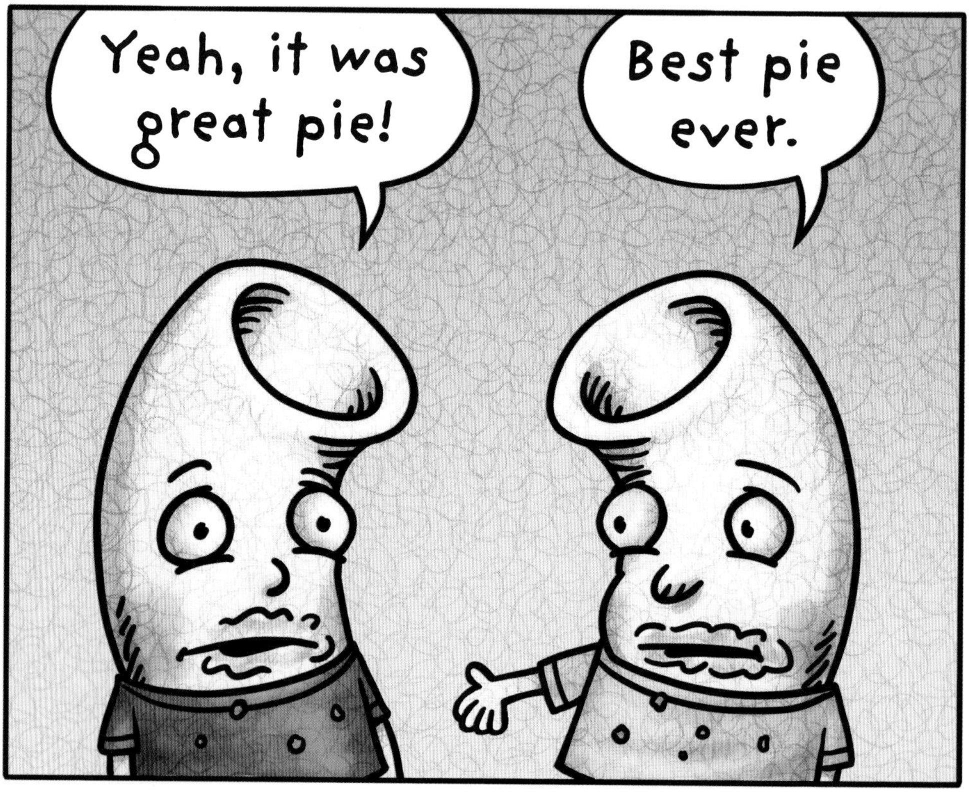
Yeah, it was great pie!
Best pie ever.

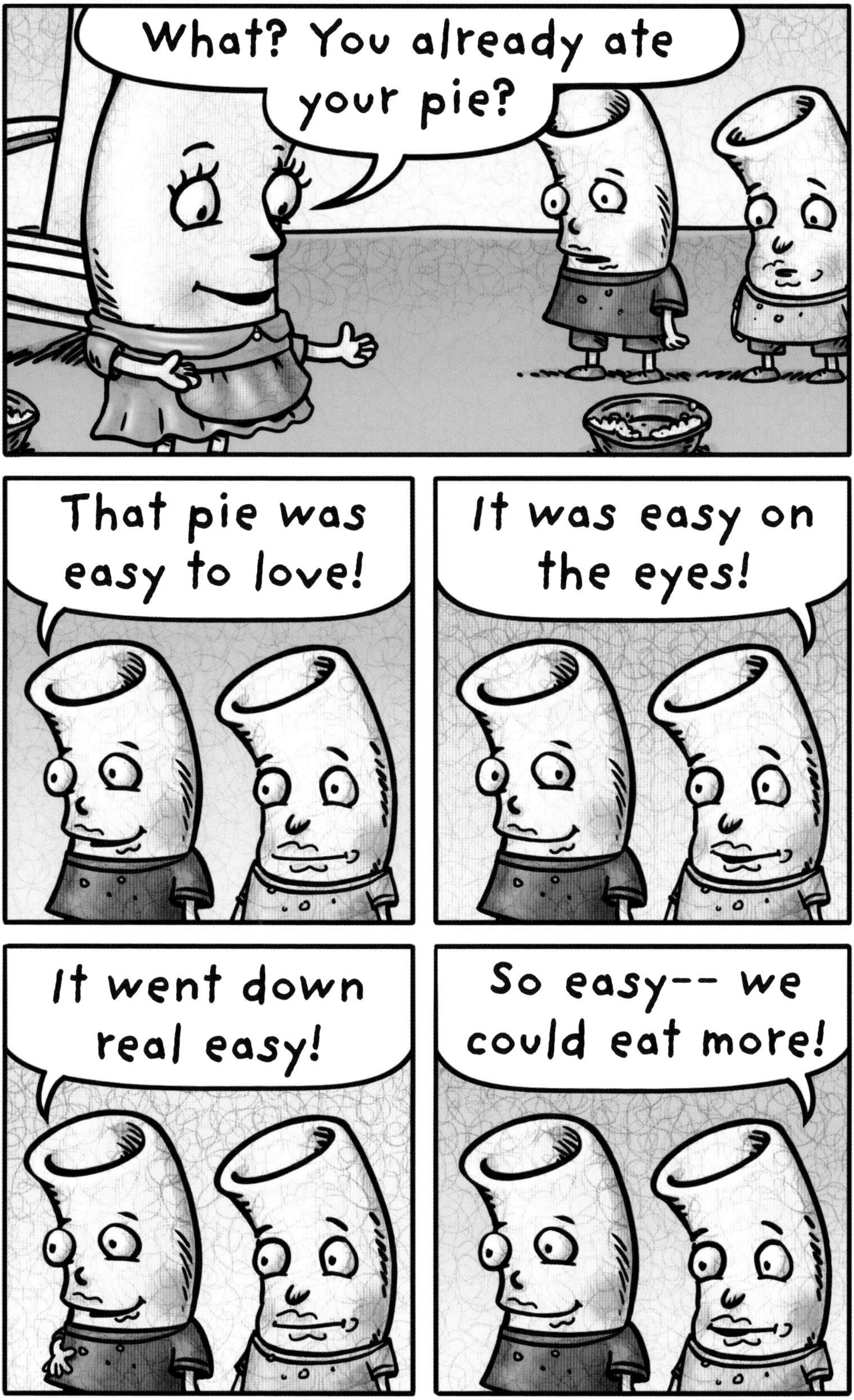
What? You already ate your pie?
That pie was easy to love!
It was easy on the eyes!
It went down real easy!
So easy-- we could eat more!

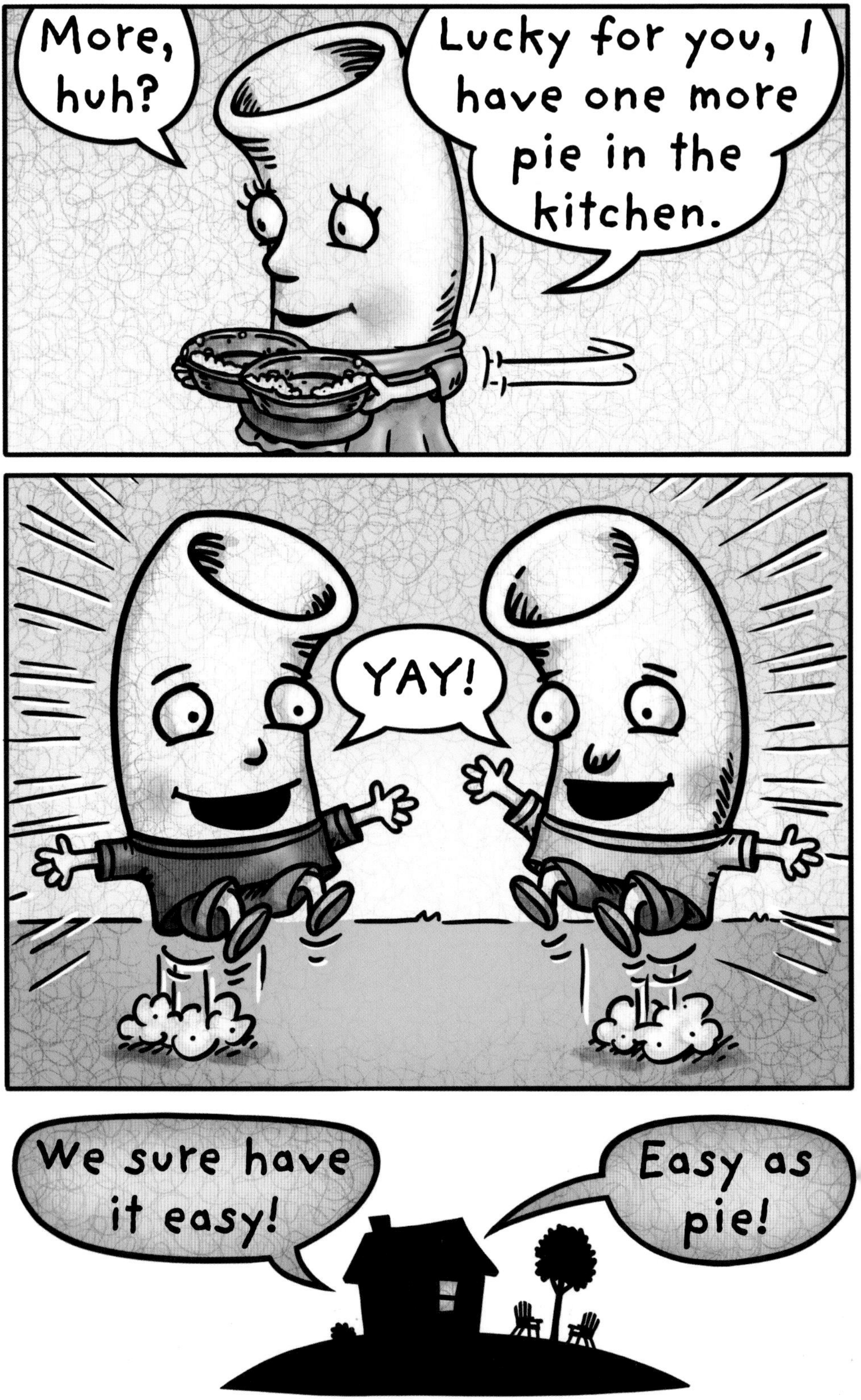
More, huh?
Lucky for you, I have one more pie in the kitchen.
YAY!
We sure have it easy!
Easy as pie!

Authors' Notes

Story Sources for Noodleheads Take It Easy

Old tales about fools, who were also called "noodles" or "noodleheads," are the inspiration for Mac and Mac's adventures in our Noodleheads series. In 1888, W. A. Clouston wrote a scholarly book called *The Book of Noodles* in which he described numerous stories that had been told for hundreds of years and quite a few dating back over two millennia. People around the world tell similar stories about their particular fools, such as Giufà in Italy, Nasr-ed-Din Hodja in Turkey, Juan Bobo in Puerto Rico, and Jack in England. These world tales remind us of our shared humanity; we have all done or said something foolish, and the stories give us a chance to laugh at ourselves. In spite of their foolishness, things usually turn out fine in the end for the fools in these old tales, perhaps because they are generally kind and well-meaning. Children find comfort in the fact that a foolish mistake usually doesn't mean the end of the world. Even if Mac and Mac don't learn from their mistakes, children who read about their adventures do. Noodlehead stories also help them understand humor, logical thinking, and the importance of distinguishing between what's true and what's a lie. Children quickly see that they should not always believe what they hear, especially when the source is a bully like Mac and Mac's "frenemy," Meatball, or Uncle Ziti, who loves to tell tall tales.

The motifs to which we refer in the information that follows are from *The Storyteller's Sourcebook: A Subject, Title, and Motif Index to Folklore Collections for Children* by Margaret Read MacDonald, first edition (Detroit: Gale, 1982), and second edition by Margaret Read MacDonald and Brian W. Sturm (Detroit: Gale, 2001). Tale types are from *A Guide to Folktales in the English Language* by D. L. Ashliman (NY: Greenwood, 1987).

Introduction

The motif that inspired this anecdote is J1925 *Hunting the lost object outside. Too dark to search for object in house where it was lost.* A version from the Middle East can be found in *Wisdom Tales from Around the World* by Heather Forest (Atlanta, GA: August House, 1997, pp. 62-63).

Chapter One: Easy as Pie???

The idea for Otto Krumb, the grocer, came from the Scottish folk song and nursery rhyme "Aiken Drum." Many children in the United States are familiar with the version by Raffi. Mary's song was inspired by the folk song "The Old Gray Mare." Using a tune from a folk song, children in the schoolyard, on the school bus, or at camp often make up alternative words. "Greasy Grimy Gopher Guts," which has the same tune as "The Old Gray Mare," is just one example of the "gross-out" type, as noted in numerous studies of children's folklore such as *Greasy Grimy Gopher Guts: The Subversive Folklore of Childhood* by Josepha Sherman and T. K. F. Weisskopf (Atlanta: August House, 1995). There's no doubt that children somewhere are creating brand-new lyrics at this moment. . . .

Mac and Mac's idea for how to lighten the mare's load came from motif J1874.1 *Rider takes the meal sack on his shoulder to relieve the donkey of his burden* and tale type 1242A *Carrying the load to spare the horse.* "The Wise Fools of Gotham," a folktale from England, in Mitch and Martha's

Noodlehead Stories: World Tales Kids Can Read and Tell (Atlanta: August House Publishers, 2000, pp. 23-25), includes this incident.

Chapter Two: Making Easy Hard

The main theme in this chapter is common in folklore regarding fools: J2700-2749 *The easy problem made hard*. The idea for Mom's story about Mac and Mac's argument about their hamsters came from motif J2722 *Telling their horses apart*. Mitch and Martha's retelling of a folktale from the midwestern United States, "Whose Horse Is Whose?", can be found in *Noodlehead Stories: World Tales Kids Can Read and Tell* (Atlanta: August House Publishers, 2000, pp. 38-39).

The second story that Mac and Mac's mom tells is motif J2161.1 *Jumping into the breeches*, also tale type 1286. This story is usually one incident in "The Three Sillies," a common world tale in which the main character is stunned by someone's silliness and sets out to find three more people who are equally silly.

The rain/pond incident was inspired by a story about Jean Sot (Foolish John), the classic fool of Cajun folktales. A short version, "Foolish John and the Rain," can be found in "Louisiana Tales of Jean Sot and Bouqui and Lapin," by Calvin Claudel, Southern Folklore Quarterly, Vol. 8, No. 4, 1944, p. 299.

Chapter Three: Easy Come, Easy Go

The idea for the events in this chapter came from "The Wolf and the Mink," a story told by Elaine Grinnell, an elder of the S'Klallam (native people of Washington state), found in *Trickster: Native American Tales*, edited by Matt Dembicki (Golden, CO: Fulcrum, 2010, pp. 89-102). The motif is K401.1 *Dupe's food eaten and then blame fastened on him.* In the tale, Mink, who is starving, catches and cooks two fish. Wolf, who has smelled the cooking, shows up just as Mink is about to eat. All creatures have been taught that they must share if a friend arrives at mealtime. Mink doesn't want to share, so he tells Wolf that he is not going to eat his fish right away. Wolf knows that Mink is lying and begins to tell a long, boring story until Mink falls asleep. After Wolf eats the fish, he puts bits of fish skin on Mink's lips and pokes fish bones between his teeth. When Mink awakes, he wonders where Wolf went—and then where his fish went. However, he then tastes fish on his lips and finds the bones in his mouth. Concluding that he really enjoyed his meal, Mink heads home, quite contented.

This book offers opportunities to familiarize children with several idioms/sayings such as "That's easy as pie," "Easy peasy," "She's on Easy Street," "That's as easy as falling off a log," "Pie in the sky," "Everything's just peachy," "Easy on the eyes," and "It went down easy." For example, "easy as falling off a log" refers to the difficulty of standing on a log that is floating in water. The saying began when it was common for trees to be cut down and put into a river where they would float down to a mill. Lumberjacks soon came up with contests to see who could stand on a log the longest time. If children are not familiar with log rolling, demonstrate the difficulty by showing this news report of a ten-year-old girl teaching an adult male how log rolling is done: https://www.youtube.com/watch?v=38bv-GBijFY.

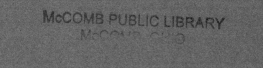

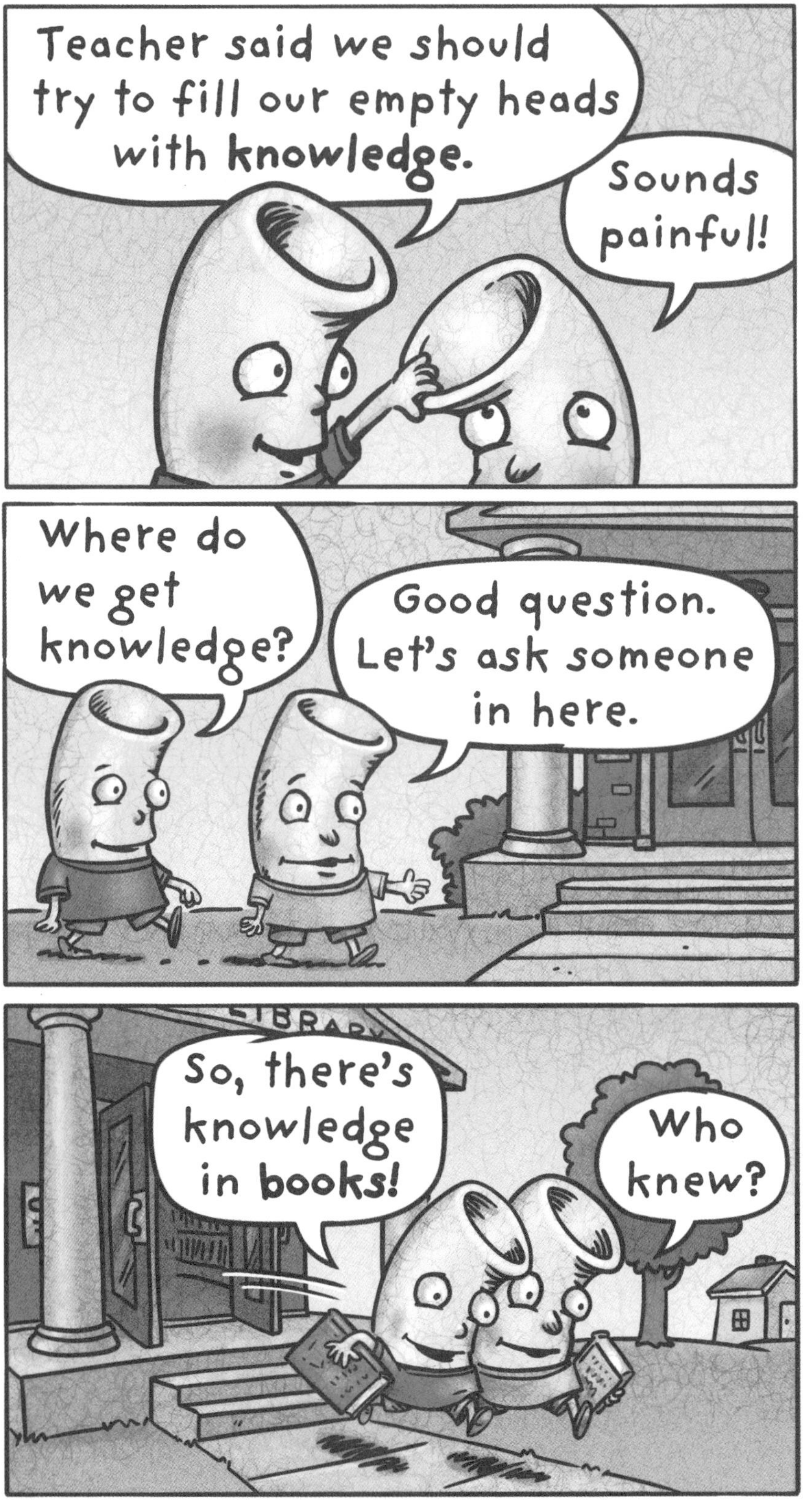
Teacher said we should try to fill our empty heads with **knowledge**.
Sounds painful!
Where do we get knowledge?
Good question. Let's ask someone in here.
So, there's knowledge in **books**!
Who knew?